Fox and Wolf

Apex Investigations: Book One

Julia Talbot

CONTENTS

Fox and Wolf

Apex Investigator Dylan is just the man for the job when a werefox comes to the agency needing help after the murder of a client. He has no idea what a can of worms he's opening when his boss assigns him the case, though.

Ever since finding the dead body of one of his clients, foxy Rey Mercier's life is a mess, and he needs help desperately. He has no idea why he's the target a ruthless killer, and he hopes Dylan and his motley crew of shifters at Apex Investigations can help him find out. Dylan and Rey have to deal with literal corporate tigers and dire crocodiles shifters... all while deciding what to do about the mate bond that's becoming undeniable. And is that even possible between fox and wolf?

Apex Investigations Reading Order

Fox and Wolf

Jaguar and Grizzly

Mountain Lion and Bobcat

Alpha and Bear

To my encouragement, beta reader, and fan, my wife, BA Tortuga.

To Jaymi, who keeps track of names and places and isn't afraid to tell me the truth.

ONE

The minute the fox walked in his door, Mick Hartness knew he was going to be trouble. The guy was a ginger, after all, and they were always, always full of surprises, and not the good kind. This client wasn't going to be a "here's chocolates and flowers" kind of shocker. No, he was going to be "hey, I'm a serial killer." That was the way of things for a private investigator, though. When you worked for other shifters, you never knew what you'd get.

Mick stood, holding out a hand to shake. "Mr. Mercier. Pleasure. Please, have a seat and tell me what I can do for you." He had an idea, because his assistant, Carrie, usually got a few details, but Apex Investigations Inc. was ever discreet. He only got in detail in person.

The shake was firm, but the little man's hand was sweaty, and the look in the copper eyes was worried. "Nice to meet you, Mr. Hartness. You come highly recommended."

"Thank you." They settled, and Mick waited for the knock on the door. Carrie always offered drinks and snacks, so there was no sense in starting before she did.

The tap was gentle, then his favorite she-wolf on the face

of the earth came in. "Can I get anyone anything? Coffee? Water?"

"Can I please have a cup of coffee, ma'am?" Oh, Mercier was polite and jittery. Nice.

"Of course. Cream or sugar?" She smiled gently. Carrie was all maternal instinct.

"Black is fine. Thank you, ma'am."

"Mick?"

"The usual." He took his with cream and half a dozen sugars. And with cookies. Peanut butter. He needed his energy.

"I'm on it." She let herself out, closing the door behind her.

Mercier stared at him, so Mick cleared his throat. "So, I understand you're under some sort of threat? Can you give me some idea what we're dealing with?"

"I'm an information broker. I sell what I know. It's weirdly like what you all do, right?"

"Right. I guess that can be a hazardous profession, just like mine." Mick smiled, humoring the guy.

"Exactly. I was hired to retrieve a file from a corporation for an individual and, somehow, I've fallen into a bit of trouble." Mr. Mercier's face took on a strained expression.

"What kind of trouble? A vague description here is no one's friend."

"To be honest, I'm not exactly sure. After the file—a quite physical one, mind you—was delivered, I began to receive emails begging me to come pick it up from my client. I agreed, and when I went to get the papers to replace them?" Mercier shuddered. "She was dead. Drowned in her pool."

"So, someone killed your client for, what? The files you got for her??"

"No. No, the files she'd requested were her own HR record. What could have been in those files worth killing for?"

"Huh." Mick sat back, steepling his fingers under his chin. "You found her?"

"Yes." The fox went pale as milk. "She was frantic. I read those files. There was nothing in there. Nothing of importance."

"Okay. So what happened then?" He didn't have to take notes. He had a great memory. Really great. Anything Rey Mercier told him would be stored away in his very own hard drive.

"I ran. I went home. Then the phone calls started, the texts, the emails, threatening me if I didn't return the files. I don't have them."

"You had returned them from your client's house, yes?" Something wasn't adding up here. What would be so important in an HR file to kill someone over?

"No. No, I returned them to the corporation, by the way."

Mick shook his head, confused. "Okay. Let me see if I have this straight. Your client asked you to get her HR files from a company she had previously or did now work for. You gave them to her, and she began getting calls and threats. So she called, asked you to take them back to the company. When you came to do that, she was dead?"

"I returned the files as soon as I could. I didn't really know what to do, since she was dead."

"Why paper?" Mick asked. No one was solely paper anymore. It was foolish, ridiculous. Utterly silly.

"The company didn't give me an option. I think they were manipulating data but didn't want any trail. I don't know why they couldn't send a PDF or something, but this was a weird legal situation, which was why I was called in as a secure courier, which is also a service I provide."

"Like handcuffing a briefcase to your wrist?"

"Exactly so."

Mick wasn't sure why someone would hire this little man for something that required security. He didn't seem the type.

"And you're sure you didn't take anything else from the company HR office?" He knew exactly who he would be turning this case over to, but he needed to have all the t's crossed and i's dotted in the interview first.

Carrie tapped on the door, returning with coffees and sweets.

"Thank you." He smiled at her, and she winked. She loved playing like she wasn't half the brains of their operation. Mick would be lost without her.

"Of course. I brought extra cookies. They're delicious."

"Thank you, ma'am," Mercier muttered.

"They really are good cookies," Mick said when Carrie left. "Peanut butter. Looks like oatmeal raisin too."

"I love raisins." Mercier's nose twitched, scenting the food.

"Well, here. I'm a peanut butter fiend." Mick turned the plate so oatmeal raisin was on the fox's side of the desk.

"Thank you."

Mick heard the snarl of Mercier's stomach. Hmm. Someone was a little desperate. Maybe Rey Mercier had been on the run, and that was why his chickens seemed so scattered.

"Would you like something more substantial? I can have Carrie order in sandwiches while we wait for Dylan. That's your investigator."

"No. No, this is lovely. Thank you." Hunger gleamed in Mercier's eyes for a moment, though.

Mick grabbed his phone under the desk, texting Carrie quickly. "Subs and chips."

"Yes, boss."

"Can you help me?"

"Of course. We'll help look into it." Mick tilted his head, scenting a tiny hint of fear. "Do you have a place to stay?" He would need to put someone on safe-house duty if the guy was in a hotel or something.

"I've been driving. My apartment isn't safe."

Rey meant sleeping in his car. "Okay. Well, as much as I hate to, I need to talk budget." Hourly billing added up. People didn't think about it, but it was so true.

"Of course. I'm willing to pay to find out who's doing this."

"Here's a listing of our rates." Mick found it easier to hand over a piece of paper. Boom, all in writing and set in stone so his clients could read it.

"Do what you need to." Rey set the paper aside with no more than a cursory glance.

Damn. Carte blanche. He hoped the guy meant it, because this job could be expensive.

"Okay." Mick sat back in his chair again, grabbing his coffee so he could contemplate. "I want to call in Dylan, get him digging. Do you mind meeting with us both?"

"No, of course not." Mercier nibbled a cookie, watching him closely.

"Thanks. That helps, all of us being on one page." Mick tugged out his phone again, this time obviously, so he could text Dylan. He fucking hated trying to figure out the unbelievably complicated desk phone Carrie had forced on him. Honestly, what did they need those things for?

Dylan knocked on the door only a few moments later, and damn, Mick was relieved. Time to turn this interview over to the investigator, and he couldn't think of anyone better to take it on than his resident ex-cop.

Two

Dylan walked into his boss's office, eyebrows lifting at the cozy scene. Cookies and coffee. A sharp, copper-all-over fox shifter. Mick looking scowly. Yay.

"Boss. You rang?"

"I did. Meet your new client. Rey Mercier, meet Dylan Weems. Dylan. Rey."

Mercier stood, held out one hand to shake.

"Mr. Mercier." He shook hands. No calluses, but not soft. The grip was firm but quick, as if Mercier was unused to touching, or maybe intimidated by him.

Either way, Mercier was nervous.

He sat, intrigued by the nerves, by the buzz of energy. The little man made his nose work, made his hand tingle where they touched.

Mick smiled, but it was strained, more predatory than anything.

Dylan stifled a grin of his own. Mick was really ill-suited to schmoozing with the clients. He could only do it for so long before getting antsy.

The door popped open again, Carrie coming in with a big bag from the sub shop downstairs. "Working lunch!"

Oh, a big enough client for sandwiches. Impressive. The budget must be good on this one.

Dylan grinned at Carrie. "Cheesesteak?"

"Two footlongs. Spicy Italian for the boss. I got a variety you might like, Mr. Mercier. Cheese and veggie, or tuna, or turkey and provolone. Or all three. There are chips and pickles in the other bag."

A rush of hunger seemed to pour from Mercier, and Dylan felt the hair on the back of his neck raise at the scent. What the heck was that all about?

"I'd like to pay for lunch," Mercier said, reaching for his wallet.

"Nonsense! I'll expense it to your new account." Laughing merrily, Carrie left the room, closing them in with the food.

Mick doled out sandwiches. Two each for them, three six-inch subs to Mercier. "Eat any and all. For real."

Ah, so it was like that, was it? Someone was starving.

Mercier took one of the sandwiches and unwrapped it with shaking fingers.

He was trying hard not to devour it and make a mess, Dylan thought. He and Mick both bent their heads over their food, giving Mercier a little time to hoover in that first sandwich and bag of chips. Then they could all relax and stop wanting to guard their resources like the canids they were.

He spent a few minutes surreptitiously checking the fox out. Mercier was running on fumes—dark circles and twitching nose proving that. The shirt was clean but not pressed, and the man's sneakers were blown.

Clearly, he was clean and he had enough cash to expense their services, so his condition meant he was scared. Unable to light in one place for fear of getting caught.

"So, what information do you need from me? I don't

know where we would even begin." Mercier pushed his hair behind his ear.

Dylan looked to Mick.

"Someone thinks he stole information he doesn't have, is the short answer."

"Okay, then I start by retracing your steps. I need to know about any corporations involved so I can see what sorts of trade they do." Dylan started ticking off things on his fingers.

"Pearson Inc. is the business involved. PR work, mostly for politicians, businessmen, etc. My client was Elise Barker. She's... gone."

"Politicians and big business...." He and Mick exchanged a nod. "That's always trouble."

"It was a simple job. Nothing dangerous."

"Of course, but what did you know about your client?" Dylan smiled a little, knowing he was far more approachable than Mick with his shaggy hair and more craggy than sharp face. "She could have been involved in any number of things for the company."

"All I did was retrieve her HR file. Simple, straight-forward."

"I'd still like to retrace your steps, if only virtually. Our first action is to get you a safe place to stay." He noticed Rey had gone for the turkey and provolone, then the cheese and veg. The tuna stayed wrapped up.

If he didn't eat it, Brock or James would take it from the fridge later. Kitties and their damn tuna.

"I'll be okay if I keep moving. I don't have what they're looking for. I returned everything. There was nothing in there."

"I believe you." Dylan said it in a steady, not conde-scending voice, wanting Mercier to know he really did believe it. "However, as my client, I need to know you're safe. We can move you regularly, but let us handle accommodations."

It really wasn't negotiable. He couldn't waste time following the fox around and do his job at the same time.

"Oh, I—well...."

Mick snorted. "Better not to argue with Dylan. He's stubborn."

"I'm quick more than stubborn, but I have my moments."

"I imagine so." Dylan finished up his chips, then licked his fingers, noting the way Mercier's gaze lingered when he did. Now the five-hundred-thousand-dollar question was, did Mercier covet his chips or his mouth? Probably the chips, more's the pity.

"I vow I didn't do anything to cause this. I don't have the file they want."

"Good. That will make it easier. It's harder when the client isn't being honest." Dylan stood. "Come on back to my office. I'll get you to write out names and such, and then I can work on the basics while you get some rest."

"All right. It was good to meet you, Mr. Hartness." Mercier stood and held one hand out to Mick.

"You too. Good luck to you." Mick slipped the tuna sub off the desk. He was probably thinking of their kitties too.

"Thank you." Mercier followed Dylan, steps absolutely silent behind him.

He could understand why this guy would be used for stealth. And he would be the kind to sit quietly in a corner and record everything. Yeah, a good information broker. Dylan let Mercier into his office, then indicated the chair across from his desk.

Mercier sat gingerly, bright eyes shining at him.

"Okay, so I'm gonna say something I used to say all the time when I was a cop." He plopped into his chair. Leaning, he steepled his fingers under his chin. "You're gonna get sick of me asking the same questions over and over. Unlike a perp, I'm not trying to catch you in a lie. I'm trying to find every angle, every bit of information you don't even know you have."

Those eyes didn't miss much, he'd bet. Such a gorgeous color.

"Information is my life. Ask away."

"How did your client come to hire you?" Dylan tugged a legal pad out of his desk, then grabbed a pen. Unlike Mick, he couldn't remember anything unless he wrote it down.

"She contacted me via a client of mine—a young man that uses me for research."

"So it was word of mouth. Do you think he'd be willing to speak to me?" He'd learned to write without really glancing down years ago. What the interviewee's face said told Dylan as much as their words.

"I'll call him. I don't see why not. I don't want him put in danger, though. He's a dear friend."

"No. I can meet with him over the phone, if need be, and make it as anonymous as possible. In fact, I'll have you call him from a burn phone I provide." A dear friend. Why did Dylan feel a tiny spurt of... what? Anger? Jealousy?

"That's fine. I just hate thinking I got him hurt."

"Of course." He tapped his pen on the pad. "And what did she do at the corporation?"

"She had been a public relations specialist for a senator. He had a PR crisis involving a relationship with an underage girl. She was fired."

"I see." He did see. He had to research the senator and the girl. He scribbled, fascinated in spite of himself. Dylan loved puzzles, loved how everything fit together when it shouldn't, or shattered when he tried to force it to fit.

He watched Mercier, the fox sitting perfectly still and somehow constantly moving at the same time. The exhaustion was getting to the man, he could tell. He could see it written on the fox like glow-in-the-dark ink.

So he asked a question or two more, but he had enough to start with. Time to let the guy rest. Then go get that tuna sandwich before kitties did, because he was still starving.

"Here, Mr. Mercier—"

"Rey, please. I feel weird being mistered."

"Sure. Here, at the back of the office." He rose, showing Mercier to his little wonder room. They each had one in their office, which showed how Mick got the kind of work they did. There was a sink, a rolling closet, and a twin bed, as well as a bookshelf of reading material. "The blankets are all freshly washed. Please, rest up while I start making calls. You're safe here."

"Really?" The man's face began to elongate, the fox right at the surface.

"Really. Seriously, curl up. Fox out, if you need to." He stepped back, allowing Rey into the room. God, he knew how that felt, being too tired to cope. After years of being a cop, he knew how it felt to sit in a car too many days in a row. Never fun.

Rey moved to the bed and curled up on the mattress. Dylan would bet his bottom dollar that there would be a fox there in minutes, sleeping hard.

He didn't stay to watch, even if he was obsessed with how other shifters worked their change. Dylan's hurt. Every time. Rey was even more fascinating than others too. So he couldn't watch.

Instead, he went to the breakroom, hunting....

Damn.

"Hey, James."

The big golden-haired mountain lion shifter nodded, munching the tuna sandwich. "Mmmph."

That was totally unfair. His mouth had been set on that sandwich.

James jerked his chin to one side and swallowed. "There's

at least two more bags of sandwiches. Carrie had more brought up when she realized we were all in."

"Oh God." Damn. He found the bags, pulling out an Italian and a tuna. "Hallelujah."

"You got two hollow legs, Dylan. Swear to God."

"I do. I was premature and I never really feel caught up." He unwrapped the sandwiches, then added chips.

"*Comida.*" Their colleague Brock joined them and grabbed a huge pile of food.

"So, what you got on your plate, Dylan?" James asked. "I saw the little redhead."

"Hot as hell. Smelled exhausted, though. Seriously." Brock was a horndog and a half, but there was a weird wariness in his eyes when he talked about Rey.

"He is. He's asleep in my office." Carrie would never let anyone get past her, so he felt fine leaving Rey in there. She wouldn't let Rey out either. "Political, I think."

"Ah man, those ones suck."

"I like them," Brock said.

"You would," James growled.

"Easy, pussycats. We don't need to fight." Although Dylan had to admit, it was a pretty visual.

Brock just gave them a cream-licking smile. "Mmm. Tuna. Lots of it. Carrie must be in full-moon mode."

"Hey, you're eating one too," James pointed out.

"The little fox went for turkey and veggie." Mick leaned against the doorframe. "He sleeping, Dylan?"

"Yep. What did you make of him, boss?" Dylan asked.

"Nervy. Tired. He's been living in his car. I do buy that he has no idea why someone is after him. You can tell he thought this was a simple run-and-dump courier gig. Get anything else from him?"

Dylan shook his head. "Just a few people to contact."

"I hate when someone starts out dead. It's tough to question them." Mick rolled his eyes.

"No shit. She was in PR for a politico and there was an underage affair. I wonder if there wasn't blackmail involved. As in, he had no idea he was bringing her more than her file...." People got very, very pissy when money got involved.

"That makes sense, but it also complicates the hell out of things. Senator Cooper, I take it?"

How did Mick always know this shit? The man was connected so deep Dylan wondered if he was a tree instead of a wolf. Roots all over the place.

"I'll start digging. I wanted—" Another sandwich. "—to give Mercier a chance to fall asleep."

"Shit, I came for another bite." Mick sat with them. "Tell me there's more cheesesteak."

"And more cookies," Brock said. They all knew about the boss's colossal sweet tooth.

"Oh hooray, cookies." Mick grinned over, pure big bad wolf. "Good job, by the way, keeping Mercier in the building. He wanted to run bad."

"Where did he think he was going to go?" Dylan asked. For goddess' sake, Rey had come to them for help.

Mick grabbed food. "I guess to his car so he could keep moving. He wasn't thinking clearly. It was obvious his reserves were spent."

"Oh, poor baby." James purred softly, eyes flashing.

Brock sighed. "Kitty, you're such a mother hen. He's a fox. He'll come out of this just fine. You better watch out, Dylan. They invade other creatures' dens and take them over."

"Bitchy poo," James said with another growl.

"What? It's true. They're like rodents." Brock snapped his teeth together.

"They hunt," James pointed out. "They're canids."

"Sure. Whatever." Brock could roll out that *everrrrrr*

longer than anyone else Dylan knew. South American kitty. Did they even have foxes there?

"Are you just being a hater because James was all 'oh poor cute red fox'?" Mick kept a straight face asking it.

Impressive.

Brock growled softly. "Like I give a shit what James thinks."

James stood, blinking coldly across the table. "You want to take this outside?"

"No." Mick barked out the word, slamming his hand on the table. "You two behave. The client is still in the building."

Both cats gave the boss a sullen look individually, but they backed down.

"Did I miss something?" Kit, their resident bear shifter, filled the whole doorway.

"Oh, sweet bear. You're the king of missing the drama." Dylan shook his head, smiling over. "Hungry?"

"Yes. Fox shifter?"

"Yep. He's in trouble." Dylan loved this team of misfits and weirdos. The situation was even better than being a cop, because they all worked together, and their caseload never got too heavy.

"Smells like worry and tired." God, there was nothing like that ursine sniffer. Nothing.

"Got it in one. James, I'll email you a list of stuff for you to check."

James was their computer whiz, the one who could find out your shoe size and the brand of condoms you preferred.

"Excellent. You know I love having something to do. Just point me and shoot me."

"I will." Dylan scooted over to make room for Kit.

The bear sat, leaning into him in greeting, nose pressing to his for a moment. Mick had found Kit as an adolescent, and they'd watched him grow up into a happy, basically well-adjusted member of their little pack.

Dylan rubbed noses, then turned back to his snack. Second lunch? Whatever. They weren't hobbits.

Kit grabbed the cookies, humming happily over the snack. "So good."

"There's tuna," Brock murmured.

"Later. I have a meeting in twenty. No tuna breath." Kit waved his hand in front of his face.

Mick grinned at Kit, the heavy laugh lines growing deeper. "Good man."

"I try, boss. Anyway, the fox will need watching. He's nervous enough to try to bolt. I can smell it." Kit's sense of smell was better than even Dylan's and Mick's, and that was saying something.

"He's going to sleep. I mean, who would try to get past Carrie?" Dylan grinned when that got a chuckle.

"A man who's scared he's getting people hurt." That was Mick.

"True enough," James agreed.

Dylan sighed, taking another handful of cookies to tide him over in his office. "Looks like I'm back to work."

"Have fun. Email me deets."

"Did you just say 'deets,' James?" Dylan stared at the guy, worried he was spending too much time online.

"I did." James batted those ridiculously long gold eyelashes at him.

"Cats." He chuckled, then stuffed a peanut butter cookie in his mouth.

"Meow."

Dylan laughed all the way back to his office. When he checked, Rey Mercier was still asleep, his huge fluffy tail curled over his nose.

The clothes were all carefully folded up at the foot of the

bed, waiting for Mercier to wake back up. Good deal. Dylan sat at his computer. He shot some notes off to James, then pondered his next move. Oddly, he really wanted to go curl up with Rey. Like, a lot. As in, the urge was so strong it unnerved him. Ridiculous, but sometimes wolves could be. He knew this.

Shaking it off, he pulled out his notebook and pen, then got to work. He had enough to go on for now. The rest would come out in the wash. It always did.

THREE

Rey woke in a strange place, eyes flying open, his nose working overtime. Wolves. Bears. Cats? Cats. Oil. Computers. Tuna fish. Peanut butter.

Oh. The private investigators. Indeed.

He relaxed for a moment, his human eyes staring at the ceiling. Thankfully, the change didn't take him hard. He dressed silently, making sure he was totally put together before he opened the door.

"Hey there." The big shaggy wolf who'd been assigned to his case smiled at him. "Feeling a little better?"

"Yes, thank you." Rey needed a bathroom, a cup of coffee, and answers.

"There's a bathroom out in the hall. Do you want something to drink?"

Oh, blessed mind reader. "Coffee? Back in a jiff."

He hurried off and did his business, his stomach screaming at him. Then he cleaned up and headed back to the office, checking his phone on the way.

He had a few messages, but nothing he needed to answer. Thank goodness.

Right now he didn't know who to answer and who not to. Anyone could be paid to betray him. He had no friends or family, just professional acquaintances.

At this point he just needed to run and keep going.

"Have a seat," Dylan said. "Carrie is bringing coffee."

"Thank you. Have you found anything?" Rey slipped into the chair across from Dylan's desk.

"Well, Senator Cooper does have a taste for underage girls. That's who your lady was working for. It's possible she was blackmailing him, I suppose. The firm seems as on the up-and-up as any PR people can be, but there are a couple of players there who have shady backgrounds."

"Her files didn't have anything unusual. Just performance reviews, a write-up, then her exit interview."

"So you did look at the files?"

"Yes. I had to ensure they were what she requested."

"They were in standard folders? No special folio?"

"Just HR folders. Manila. I don't know why they weren't electronic files. Those are always easier." *Always.*

"See, that's why I keep thinking she had to be looking for something to show…. How soon after the drop-off did she call you?" Dylan's gaze narrowed, but it looked like thinking eyes, not accusation stare.

"You mean after the calls started? The threats?"

"You said she called you to come get the files. How soon after the drop-off?"

Dylan had said he would ask the same questions in different ways, so Rey went with it.

"Oh, not even two days. I met her with the file at noon, and she began texting the next midnight." He touched the arms of the chair, his fingers moving restlessly.

"Okay." Dylan scribbled notes. "Possible scenarios, then. Someone was supposed to send something with her files and didn't. Someone did send something with the files and you didn't know it. Or somehow you accidentally grabbed something. You notice details, so I think three is unlikely. What clothes did you wear to the pickup?"

"Khakis, a blue oxford, a navy jacket. Loafers, my lucky socks."

Amusement flashed in Dylan's dark green eyes. "You have lucky socks?"

Rey drew in a bit on himself, wondering if he was being teased. "Yes."

"Hey, not mocking. So do I. Mine have flamingos on them."

"Mine have rainbows and pots of gold." He shared a smile with Dylan.

"Cool. Have you washed the clothes?" Dylan was mostly business, but his whole demeanor was warmer. They had a common foible now.

"They're at my apartment. I don't... I'm relatively sure I didn't. I wash the socks by hand."

"Okay, we need to go get them. If something was slipped into your clothes, we need to know." Dylan stood.

"All right. I don't think it's safe. It's been pretty disarranged." In fact, *pretty much* was a bit of an understatement.

"Okay. You stay here and let me have your key." Dylan held out a hand, clearly ready to be obeyed, like the big male wolf he was.

"You're going alone? They're mean, whoever they are."

"I was a cop, Rey. I'm used to mean." Dylan's smile was back to warm. Almost sweet. "I'll get us a good coffee on the way back."

"Then I'll come. I'll sit in your car. Or something. I won't be any bother." He didn't like the idea of Dylan seeing his apartment all filthy and destroyed.

"Oh, I don't—"

Rey crossed his arms over his chest. "No key if I don't go."

Dylan stared, and he stared back. Then those pretty lips twitched. "Okay. But you have to stay in the car, and I'll park it out of sight."

"Fair enough." He'd decide what to do next once they got there.

"Okay. Come on." Dylan opened the door, where the lady, Carrie, had one hand raised to knock.

"Oops."

"Hey. We're heading to Mr. Mercier's primary address. I need to see the scene there, and his clothes."

"He's going with you?" Her eyes went wide.

"Yes." Dylan sighed, then made a universal what-are-you-going-to-do shrugging motion. "I'll take precautions."

"I'll be good. It's my home. My den, hmm? I'll know where things are."

"I know. I'm sorry it was violated."

"Cop speak." He dared to tease and got a laugh for his effort.

"You're right, but I know it sucks. Someone tossed my office at work once. Knowing we had a crooked person on staff was devastating."

Rey nodded and sighed. It had been more than devastating. His whole den smelled of... fish. It was bizarre.

They made their outside to a large SUV, one that wouldn't stand out among the soccer moms in most neighborhoods, even with the dark windows.

"That one's mine." Rey had a bright red Smart car, packed to the gills.

"I would never fit in there." Dylan was wide-eyed, staring. "We might have to do a search if we don't turn up anything at the apartment."

"There's nothing illicit in there. I swear. I grabbed what I could and ran."

"I believe you, but what if someone planted something there?"

Oh dear. He'd never even thought of that, and he was used to being cautious. Goodness.

"I— Why? It was a harmless set of files. I didn't even steal them. Someone gave them to me."

"Someone might also have lied about giving you something else to deflect from them. We'll figure it out."

Usually Rey was smart enough to figure things out. Usually he was clever. This was different, though. This was being hunted.

He was scared. Truly frightened of the faceless, nameless people stalking him. They had destroyed property. Killed his client. What else would they do?

Strangely enough, he did feel safer with Dylan. So much. Dylan made him feel... settled. At home.

Silly, because Dylan had done nothing—nothing—to prove that he was a massive protector, but it didn't matter. There was something about the man.... Maybe the way he cared enough to make sure Rey slept. Maybe it was the way his blankets smelled. Honestly, maybe Rey was just desperate enough to believe anything.

They slid into the SUV, the leather seats cradling him. How plush.

"Seat warmer?" Dylan asked.

His butt heated, and Rey laughed, clapping his hands with delight. "This is awesome."

"The boss is good to us. We do enough sitting in cars doing surveillance that he wants us comfortable."

"I guess freezing off your private parts is less than fun."

"It also sucks to sit in a hard vinyl seat." Dylan got them moving, the big machine sliding into gear so smoothly. Not at all like his little car where you felt every bump.

He could totally sleep in this car, rest. Not that it was going to happen, but it was possible.

"So, is this your first set of complications on the job?" Dylan asked.

"It's the first time I've had a client murdered." That was a good enough answer, hmm?

"Never had to go on the run?"

"No." He sighed. "I've had people I was forced to avoid, but this is very different."

Of course he'd had trouble. You didn't get into his line of work without a little danger, but the worst he tended to risk was a hysterical secretary or a client who couldn't stop chewing their nails.

These threats, a murder…. Goodness. Rey scrubbed his hands over his face. Then he jumped perhaps a mile when Dylan touched his arm.

"We'll figure it out, Rey." That deep, rumbly voice held a large measure of comfort.

"I hope so." He didn't know what he was going to do if he had to leave the country. Hell, he wasn't totally sure what he would do if he had to leave the city.

"We're good at what we do."

Dylan never had to ask for directions. So the fellow had looked up how to get to his place. Why that surprised Rey, he had no idea.

His apartment was on the nicer side of Aurora. One day he intended to relocate to Boulder or, if he hit it big, retire to Estes, but for now he was happy.

"Nice," Dylan said when they drove by his complex. "I'll park just up this hill. What unit are you?"

"230B." He pointed to one of the little condo-esque buildings. "I bet someone's watching."

He would be surveilling if he were trying to find something.

Rey looked around, trying to see in the gloom. This was his time—dawn and dusk—and he could see a crack in the glass in the front window, a series of claw marks down low on the doorframe.

Dylan was going to need him in there too. He knew what was what.

Nodding, Dylan pulled well past his place to park. "That's why I want you to stay in the car."

"No. You need me."

Dylan turned to stare at him. He would bet that expression intimidated a lot of people. Those green eyes could he very flat. Hard.

He thought it was kind of cute, honestly. It made him want to lick Dylan's nose. He'd had that urge more than once since they'd met, in fact.

"It's true. You won't know what's right or wrong, what's different."

"Then I should park right in front." Dylan sighed, a world-weary sound, before putting the vehicle back in gear. "We don't need to be running a mile if someone comes after us. I'll make it clear I'm armed. With any luck they'll think I'm a cop and leave us be."

"You read as penal officer. No worries."

"Gee, thanks." Turning at a cul-de-sac, Dylan steered them back to his apartment. "Do I smell like prison sweat?"

"No. You smell like—" He inhaled, nose twitching. "—moonlight and water."

Dylan laughed, the sound delighted. "Wow. That's way better than cop car and doughnut crumbs."

"Mmm. Doughnuts." Rey had to grin. He loved sweets. With raisins. And frosting.

"Do you like them? I know a killer shop that does pastry and good coffee. Even this late in the day, they'll have good stuff!" Dylan actually bounced. How utterly cute.

"Can we? After? I'd love that." He'd need something good after all this bother.

"I would too. We'll do it." They slid to a stop, and Dylan put a hand on his arm when he would have hopped out of the SUV. "Give it just a moment."

"Fine." He wasn't eager to go back there. Not at all.

Dylan watched everything, the rearview mirrors, the door to his apartment. He wasn't sure what signs Dylan might be looking for, but Rey watched too.

That was his job, after all. Looking at everything. He didn't see anything more than what he'd already noticed, but then he hadn't the other day either.

Dylan shook his head. "I don't like this. You know that, right?"

"Yes. You just want my clothes from the day of the pickup, correct?"

"That's it. In and out." Dylan snapped his fingers.

"Indeed. In and out. Quick as a bunny."

"Or a fox through a doggie door." Dylan winked broadly, then pulled out his phone. "In case we need pictures, so I won't have to fumble for it."

Rey grabbed his key and nodded. "Let's go." He hopped out of the car and started toward the apartment, his entire body twitching from the vibrations he was sensing in the air and along the ground. Someone was watching. Hopefully it wasn't someone with a gun.

"Hurry up, Mercier."

"Yes. Yes, hurry up." He couldn't run. That triggered the prey drive in anything that might lay in wait for them.

Dylan already had the door open.

The smell made Rey gag and step back. Rotten. Rotten fish.

"Jesus. What is that?" Dylan turned his head, those pretty eyes watering.

"I don't know. Nasty." They couldn't stay out here, but they couldn't go into *that*.

"Come on." Dylan rushed inside, barking, "Get your stuff." He started snapping pictures of the main room, then the kitchenette.

Rey headed to the bedroom, trying not to breathe as he went to the en suite to dig through his laundry. The bathtub was filled with fetid water, and he shook his head. That was... so disturbingly wrong. Rey gathered all his stuff, including his lucky socks, but his eyes kept going to the tub.

The tub with bubbles rising from it.

"Dylan...."

Dylan came to the doorway, frowning. "What the ever-loving—"

He pointed to the horrifying green water. He was fairly certain there were eyeballs.

"Get back. Out." Dylan yanked him out of the bathroom, spinning him toward the front door.

He didn't question; he ran, screeching to a halt at the sight of a huge beast in the outside doorway.

"What the fuck is that thing?" Dylan was behind him. Right behind him. Close enough to nearly knock him down.

The creature bore a long muzzle. Scales. Teeth. Black eyes.

"Croc." Goddess, they were in trouble.

"Fucking A." Dylan's gun cocked near his ear.

"Uh-huh. There's one coming from the tub." Rey was caught by the croc's faceted eyes. "Please tell me you know what to do."

"I have no idea. They're armored, kinda. I need to go for the belly or the eye."

"Uh-huh." Oh. Oh. Gracious. "The window?" He wasn't sure he could move.

"That sounds like a damn good idea. The one thing we got on them is speed."

"'Kay. Now is good. He's rather hypnotizing me."

There was no warning. The croc in front of them lunged. Dylan moved faster, tossing him at the window. Rey threw his arms up as he crashed through the glass, glad it was one big piece of thin stuff and not those old panes with all that wood.

He rolled along the grass, holding his dirty clothes against the curve of his body. *Get in the car. Come on. Stand up and move.*

Dylan landed next to him on the ground seconds later, then jumped to his feet, grabbed Rey up under one arm, and ran.

He didn't struggle, didn't fight. He just helped as best he could, like opening the car door when Dylan set him down and turned to fire a few shots across their back trail. He crawled into the car, screaming as a huge clawed hand slammed into the passenger window. "Come on!"

"Got it." Dylan ducked into the car. "Shit. Shit!"

"Start the car! Please, we must go!"

The scaly hand slammed again, the window cracking.

The engine roared to life. Dylan slapped the car into gear, squealing out backward. Rey slid into the floorboard, curling up into a tight ball.

Dylan was the expert. Rey would let him drive.

———

Dylan burned out of the parking lot, his body kind of on autopilot. Croc shifters. Like, dire ones who could move like men. Fucking A, that smell. It permeated everything.

As soon as he thought they were clear, he hit the hands-free. "Call Mick."

The phone rang twice, and then his Alpha answered with a bark. "What's wrong?"

"Two croc shifters at my client's apartment. Waiting. One in the goddamn tub. We got a problem."

"Crocs? Are you sure?"

"*Boss.*" Of course he was fucking sure.

"Sorry. That's damn rare. Okay, go to safe house three. I'll meet you there."

"Got it." Safe house three was a nice little condo in Evergreen, but they never spoke on an unsecured line about locations or driving times.

Little Rey was in a ball in the floorboard, all red fur and fuzzy tail.

He'd bet a fox could hide far better than a human. Or a wolf, for that matter.

"I expect a check-in when you're settled."

"You got it."

"Mercier?"

"Foxed out."

"Okay. I'll see what I can find on crocs. Someone will do a drive-by too, see what they can see."

"Well, proceed with extreme caution," Dylan warned. His nose twitched, the kitty-yet-canine smell of fox filling his senses. It was pleasant enough to kill the gross of croc. "Those bastards are huge and creepy."

"And stinky, if memory serves." Mick laughed roughly. "See you soon." The line went dead.

"Okay. That was good. You okay, little guy? They didn't hurt you?"

Rey bared surprisingly sharp, long teeth at him.

"Huh. Does that mean you're hurt, or I'm not allowed to call you 'little guy'?" He made three rights and a left. The white sedan wasn't following him. Good.

Rey crawled up in the passenger seat and hopped up to look out the window.

"Right. Well, we're going to a safe house. I need to stop at a McDonald's, though. Scan the car for devices." Buy about thirty hamburgers, ten twenty-piece chicken nuggets, and a small vanilla shake.

Adrenaline made him hungry, and Mick would be starving.

He imagined Rey would be hungry too. Either that or totally mindless with fear. Who knew? The guy looked pretty... calm in his fox form.

He'd actually been relatively calm in human form, if a little deer-in-the-headlights, but not a panicky idiot. Dylan was glad. The getaway was so much easier that way.

Going out the window had even been Rey's idea.

The glass had been a gamble. If it had been double pane....

Dylan pulled into the parking lot of a McD's, then grabbed his little device scanner out of the glove box. Thank God for websites like Spy Guy.

By the time he'd worked through Rey's clothes, there was a naked man in his passenger seat. He handed up the still sort of clean if a bit glass-studded khakis.

"Thanks. That was—what were those things?" Rey's eyes were huge in his thin face.

"I've heard of shifters who can do that. Be half and half. I can't."

"No. No, I can't either." Rey rolled the window down and shook out the pants.

"Good to know." Dire cave fox kinda seemed silly.... Dylan chuckled.

"I bite, you know. Hard."

"I saw those teeth of yours. Okay, we're clean." No bugs or trackers. Now food.

"Drive-through?"

"God, yes. What do you like?" He hopped back in the driver's seat, waiting for Rey to buckle in.

"Big Macs. Please."

"You got it." He ordered ten nuggets, five large fries, two Big Macs, a dozen Quarter Pounders, and a drink for him and Rey. And that shake.

By the time they got to the window, they were both buzzing, stomachs snarling.

"Unwrap me a Quarter Pounder?" He could wait on the rest, but he needed something now.

"Sure." The burger was unwrapped nice and quick, handed over as if by someone who knew how to eat on the run.

"Thanks." Dylan wolfed down the burger, feeling better the moment it hit bottom. God, he hated being ambushed.

"I'm sorry. I didn't know... I didn't even know those creatures were possible."

"Oh man, of course you didn't." He spared Rey a glance. "This is more serious than I figured, though. That kind of thing doesn't come cheap."

"Good thing I live in my car, I suppose?"

"You don't need to, and once this is over, you can... get another apartment." That place would need to be bombed to get that smell out.

"Yes. I'll probably have to do that."

"I bet." He steered onto the highway.

Rey didn't eat; he sat there, head down, nose twitching.

"You okay?" He thought the food smelled fine.

"Of course I am."

"You were hungry a moment ago, honey." That stillness worried him.

"I know. Adrenaline, I suppose."

"Sure." Dylan handed Rey a Coke. "The sugar will help."

"I'm sorry. I didn't do it, I swear."

"Do what? Honey, if you knew who these people were, you would know about the crocs."

"Yes. Gracious." Rey sipped the Coke, color slowly creeping back into the lean face.

Poor guy. Not everyone was made for this shit. Dylan did this work because he wasn't good at anything else. Too many years as a cop to not be danger wolf.

"I've been in some tight spots, even been beat up pretty badly, but... nothing like that. I'm glad you were there."

"Me too. Eat. Have some fries if the meat is too much right now." Carbs good. Beating up the fox bad. The idea made him growly, in fact. Very protective and kinda like he wanted to find whoever had hurt his fox—His? He wanted to hurt them too.

"I'm pretty omnivorous." Rey nibbled on a chicken nugget.

"Raisins, the boss said." He winked. "I bet Mick brings more cookies."

"I love raisins, yes."

"Cool. We'll grab some stuff at the store when we're settled."

"Okay. I just... I can't even begin to find words. That was... intense." Rey ate another chicken nugget. "You want one?"

He looked at his hand. The burger was gone. "Yeah. Yeah, thanks."

"Sure. You expended a lot of muscle twitch energy."

"I did?" He chuckled. "It seemed like slow motion. It's always that way when my gun is out."

"I was caught. Those eyes." Rey shivered. "God, they were... did you notice or was it just me?"

"I didn't look. You told me how you were hypnotized, so I avoided it." Dylan took the nugget Rey handed over.

"Oh, good. We might have been terribly fucked otherwise, in the bad way."

"You know it. Never look a reptile in the eye." Dylan

munched a couple more nuggets, laughing at Rey saying *fucked*. "Eat something else, man."

"A dire crocodile. Where on earth do you find a dire crocodile?"

"Direct mail? Get it? Dire-ect?" Dylan hooted, and damn if Rey didn't snort-chuckle.

That was enough to let Rey relax, breathe, and eat a hamburger.

They pulled up at the safe house maybe fifteen minutes later, and Dylan parked around back. He and Mick would switch vehicles, so no one would have seen the one he was using with Rey.

"Are you going to leave now? I mean, after we go in?"

"No. Not now. If I have to go do some leg work, someone else will come stay with you." Dylan checked all his danger areas before leading Rey in the back of the unit. The condo was great that way, with ways to get in and out without being seen. He would like a unit like that to live in, but damn if he could afford it.

Still, he fully intended to spend a couple of days working in luxury here, trying to figure out what the actual fuck.

He would put in all the virtual legwork he and James could do before he hit the streets again. It had been a mistake to run before knowing what he was getting into.

He admitted, he hadn't honestly believed that someone was trying to murder Rey. Scare him? Hurt him, yes. Murder? No.

Those crocs were out to do damage. They didn't care about the smell, about leaving a trace. They had been ready to eradicate this fox.

He had to admit, he had to wonder what Rey had really done. No one was chased like this without reason. No one spent the kind of money to have someone killed over a human resources file.

So what did he have?

"Do you have anything from the office you picked up and dropped off at? Anything at all? Even a business card?"

"I have my contact there. He and I have known each other a long time. He's in my phone, of course."

"What the hell could it be that they wanted so bad?" He held up a hand after unlocking the door. "Stay here. If you see someone coming who's not Mick, fox out and run."

"Fair enough." Rey watched him with those preternaturally bright eyes.

He did a quick check of the condo, then called Rey in. "We're good." The place was clean as a whistle, and no one seemed to be on their back trail.

Rey handed over the clothing and food to him and then began exploring, zipping through the entire place. Okay, that was impressive. The fox could move.

Also, Dylan liked that Rey wanted familiarity. Bathrooms, bedrooms, exits. Rey checked it all out. Twice.

"Come sit. We'll go over it again while we wait for Mick."

Rey came over and curled up into a heavy stuffed chair, staring at him. "Okay, ask away."

"You want your Coke?" He was gonna eat some more, but he felt weirdly self-conscious about it if Rey had nothing.

"Please. Can I have the other Big Mac? I didn't want to eat and make you watch."

"I'm totally gonna eat more."

Dylan brought their feast to the couch, handing over Rey's Big Mac and fries. Mick would just have to eat alone if they were done.

"Thank you." Watching Rey eat was fascinating—neat and precise, tiny little quick bites. Dylan couldn't stop watching, couldn't stop staring at the fox's mouth. Those lips fascinated him, made his skin too tight and hot. Not that he should be looking at a client that way.

"Do I have something on me?" Rey licked his lips.

"Huh? No. No, I was just...." *Perving? Bad wolf.*

"Just?" Rey licked the corner of his mouth, and that pink tongue was... delectable.

"I'm just watching you eat. We're all slobs. You're so not." Was that a good enough excuse? "I didn't mean to make you feel weird."

"You don't. It's nice to be seen right now. Especially after... earlier."

"I hear you." He'd thought sure he'd gotten them both killed, and it was his job to protect Rey and find out what was going on. "So who did you see when you picked up the files?"

"Corde Lesman. He's my contact. A sweet bunny who's in charge of the HR library."

"Bunny? Really?" Huh. Well, bunnies weren't exactly into espionage, usually. "What about when you dropped off?"

"I gave the file back to Corde. He was heading into the office and I just gave it back."

"Where?" Not in the office? That might account for some kind of transfer, even if it was one Rey knew nothing about.

A knock sounded on the door, so Dylan rose, drawing his sidearm. "Stay down from the windows."

Usually Mick texted when he was close.

Rey curled down, shrinking back against the chair. "Be careful."

"I will." He was pretty sure it was Mick, but what if not texting was a message in itself? He peered out the window without presenting a target. Okay. Mick. No crocs. He eased the door open. "What—"

"I brought doughnuts. My phone is charging."

"Fucker. You worried me." Not scared. Totally not scared. Just worried.

"Sorry. I was juggling." Mick handed over an enormous cardboard box of doughnuts. "I smell meat."

"McD's. On the kitchen table."

"You rock. Mr. Mercier. How are you?" Mick took in Rey with a quick glance.

"A little wigged. Dylan was very brave. Can we close the door, please?"

"Sure."

Dylan shut it and locked it so Mick could go lay down doughnuts and get burgers and nuggets. Mick handed Dylan another box. "Walk me through the crocs?"

"Not much to tell. One in the tub, one in the yard out front. Probably in the bushes."

"The tub one was... nasty." Rey stared at Dylan, hardly looking at Mick. "As in Louisiana swamp water nasty."

"It totally was. Like it needed the water for its skin." Dylan shook his head. "The other one... well, I don't know. I guess he could have been in the pool or something?"

"The hot tub is around the corner." Rey nodded, then stood and began to pace. "I should call the management company so I can warn them."

"No, we'll make an anonymous call to the cops. They'll do a site visit and talk to the management." Mick seemed very sure about that.

Dylan agreed. The last thing they needed was Rey to be out there, making things more complicated.

"Okay, so long as they're warned. Murderous assassin dire crocs aren't allowed in the hot tub." Rey sounded very prim.

"Right." Mick's eyes crinkled up, and he stuffed half a Quarter Pounder in his mouth.

Dylan just nodded gravely. "Not here either. So we'll keep an eye out."

"Here the hot tub is in the garden room. No crocs—assassin or otherwise." Mick winked.

"Oh good. I like soaking well enough, but not in green slime." Rey ate a nugget.

"No dipping sauce?" Mick asked.

"In the third bag." The lady had given him a whole bag of stuff. Ketchup and mustard and barbecue and sweet and sour.

"Excellent. So, I'm going to go out on a limb and say full-time surveillance for Mr. Mercier here. Are you going to take it, Dylan, or should I bring in one of the kitties?"

"I'll take it to begin with." Dylan smiled at Rey, who looked nervous.

"I'd like that. I've had a lot of new people today. I spend the lion's share of my time online."

"Not a problem." No, this was his case, and frankly, Dylan was taking the attack personally.

"Watch yourself online. I don't want this place compromised." Mick was worried, Dylan could tell.

"He'll be careful. I'm right here."

Mick nodded. "Well, what do you need from us, Dylan?"

"Mainly James right now. He needs to set me up a few new burn phones, get me a secure hot spot." Dylan pondered. "Grocery basics, clothes for a few days."

"Send him a list?" Mick was the worst grocery shopper ever. He could go with a list that said eggs, cheese, and bread, and come back with a *Hot Rod* magazine and a zucchini. It was maddening as hell and stupidly charming.

Also, the office had a running pool going for what Mick brought next. Dylan's money was on Hot Tamales and french onion dip.

Mmm. French onion dip.

Rey blinked at him, then smiled, almost as if he knew what Dylan was thinking.

He'd bet the fox would love crisp and crunchy. In fact, he had no doubt. Chips and dip was going on the list.

Raisins. Chips. Carrots.... "Huh?"

"Focus, buddy." Mick gave him the boss glare.

"He's had a rough afternoon," Rey murmured. "Big scary dire crocigators with hypno eye action."

"They were pretty intense, boss," Dylan agreed when Mick scoffed. "Pray you never have to find out."

"Right? We survived them. Two of them. We deserve cookies. Or the doughnuts. Thank you for those, Mr. Harkness."

Mick looked at Rey. "Are you drunk?"

"No. No, of course not." Rey flushed dark and stood up. "I'm just a little giddy from adrenaline, that's all."

"You're acting a bit more... satisfied with how things are going," Mick snapped.

Rey stiffened, nose twitching. "I was reacting to Dylan teasing me. You're not yelling at him."

Dylan's eyes widened. Whoa. He hadn't said a word. Rey met his gaze head-on, silently urging him to—to what? Have Rey's back? He glanced away, not at all sure what to do. This was his boss and his client....

Rey sighed, shoulders slumping. "I'm going to charge my laptop."

Man, Rey could move fast, and his disappointment, in Dylan specifically, was palpable.

"What's your beef with the fox?" Dylan asked, keeping it quiet, because Rey had magnetically charged hearing.

"Nothing. He just seems off. Strange. And let's be honest, no one on earth is sending something like those crocs after a goddamn innocent little fox."

"Yeah, I don't get it. I went through his clothes. Nothing. The place was trashed, boss. And if this is some elaborate game to get to us, it wins the bizarro award." He thought Rey was weird because of this thing between them, this feeling that they knew each other on a cellular level.

"He has something they want. Find out what it is." Mick, on the other hand, was hard as a rock.

"I will." Dylan was sure of that. "It has to be fairly important."

"Yeah. Figure out what he's hiding, Dylan. Suss it out so we can do this job without getting killed." Mick's moss gray eyes flashed, his chin set.

"I will," Dylan repeated. "Relax, boss. I got this."

"Yeah. Yeah, I know." Mick relented, then leaned in, rubbing their shoulders together in a motion that was as old as wolf packs.

That relaxed him. Relieved him. He didn't want Mick all freaked out about his case. The boss had enough issues to deal with.

He could deal with Rey, whatever the problem. Even if the only problem was him.

Besides, he thought he and Rey got each other. Like, really, on a deep level.

"I'll see you."

"Get to work, hmm?" Mick barked out a happy laugh before disappearing out the door.

Dylan nodded to himself as much as anything, then went hunting for Rey. Just to check on him.

Rey was in the farthest end bedroom, back to a corner, the light from the laptop turning the sharp features even harder as it reflected off his face.

He tapped at the open door. "You okay?"

"Yeah. Fine. Thanks." Rey snapped out the words.

"Sure. If you get where you want some company.... Uh, I'll be in the front room. Working." With the TV on and a doughnut in hand.

"I'm sorry about the crocodiles." Rey wouldn't look at him, shoulders hunched.

"So am I. I wish we could just figure out what they think you have. Have you checked with your contact at the company?"

"I'm emailing now to see if he can call." Rey's fingers flew over the keyboard.

"Cool. Well, holler if you need me." Dylan felt... weirdly useless. He just needed to get James on all this shit.

Rey looked up at him, eyes glowing in the growing darkness.

"You sure you're okay?" He was reluctant to just leave Rey to his own devices. He thought Mick had been hard on the guy, and he felt bad.

"I'm frightened, and I've hired people who think I did this to myself, which is a bit disconcerting."

"Honey, I don't think you did this on purpose. I think someone hid something or gave you something without you knowing." He shrugged. "Mick always suspects the client. It's part of his job."

"Well, I didn't do anything wrong. There's nothing off about me either!"

"I don't think Mick gets subtlety in human relations. He sees bad guys all over."

"That's sad." Rey looked young, vulnerable, and Dylan wanted to be in the same room with the fox, not a long hallway away.

"Come sit with me, hon. It's weird to be in separate rooms." He waited for Rey to rise, and damn if he didn't, giving Dylan a soft smile. "Thank you. Those crocs got to me a little too. I'm sorry I let Mick run roughshod on you. I feel like you're safer if you're close."

"Yes. I feel better, knowing I can see you." Rey blushed but followed him into the living room.

Not to mention looking at Rey was freakishly pleasant. What the hell was with him? At least the awkwardness seemed to be over. He hated the idea that Rey was mad at him, the very thought making him restless and itchy. "Doughnut?"

"Please. They smell amazing." Rey smiled at him again,

then moved to make sure the curtains were closed. Lord knew he couldn't blame the guy. Those crocs.... And knowing someone was out to kill you was terrifying.

"They do. The boss has good taste that way." He opened the box, offering it to Rey first.

Rey took a maple log. "Oh goodness. That's amazing."

"Right?" He loved the maple, the blueberry, and the eclairs with the vanilla frosting instead of chocolate. Mick was good to him. There were apple fritters with raisins as well. So much better than cookies. "Come sit. Do you watch television?"

"Are you kidding? I'm addicted to competition TV shows."

"Oh my God. Do you like *Top Chef*?" Dylan could totally catch up.

"*Top Chef. MasterChef. Project Runway*. You name it, I'll watch it." Rey bounced, seeming much younger. "I like sci-fi too."

"Then let's mainline!" This was a luxury vacation, even if he did intend to work his ass off on Rey's behalf. He plopped on the sofa and patted the cushion next to him. Rey grinned at him, eyes lit up.

"I'm in." Rey settled smiling over at him. "Thank you. I was... losing my wits a little."

"Well, anytime you need me to help, you just say." He wasn't one to leave his client unsupported. Rey also brought out his protective side. Maybe Mick was right and it was deliberate, but he doubted it. He really, really did.

There was something about the man that called to him, balls to bones.

FOUR

ey blinked softly, trying to remember what he was doing. The television was on, but he wasn't at home and there was someone snoring beside him.

Wake up, Rey, he thought. *Wake up and figure out what on earth is going on.* He shook himself and rolled up, trying for silence.

He looked down and saw a wolf lying in a pile of clothes, sleeping.

Oh. Dylan. His wolf protector.

He nodded and padded to the bathroom, wishing he had something soft to curl up in, something to sleep in. He did slide his pants off after he found a fluffy robe. That would work.

When he came out of the bathroom, he wavered. Bedroom or back to the couch? In the bedroom he could stretch out. On the couch he would feel less alone. Dylan was there.

He gave in to his instincts and headed back to the sofa, the wolf, the false warmth of the television.

Dylan's big head lifted, that long muzzle wrinkling as that sensitive nose worked.

"Just me. I needed to take the pants off. They were hot."

Dylan blinked, those fuzzy ears swiveling. One foot came out, pawing at the cushions next to Dylan. He was a handsome wolf.

He nodded and went to sit, curling up close. His nose told him he was safe here, that he could rest. "Thank you."

The cold tip of that snout touched his leg, Dylan sighing then and putting his head back down. There was a notebook with lots of scribbles and lots of used pages. Dylan had been working hard.

Rey didn't look. He hadn't done anything wrong. He focused on rubbing Dylan, petting the wolf's heavy fur, stroking in slow, steady motions.

Another long sigh sounded, and Dylan rolled to one side, stretching out those long legs. Toes flexed, a sure sign that he was doing a good job of carding out that thick pelt.

"You're in need of a good brushing." He'd have to find a heavy brush for Dylan's grooming, though why he thought he ought to be doing that he had no idea.

Dylan rumbled, the sound almost like a complaint. He could imagine Dylan saying he'd just washed it and couldn't do a thing with it.

"I know how good it feels, brushing. Don't grump." He stroked one sensitive ear, careful not to tug.

Dylan panted, tongue lolling out as if he were laughing. Big lovely furball.

"I'll find you a brush tomorrow. I have to go get clothes and things from my car." His little Smart car was at Dylan's office, so at least he felt like it was safe.

Dylan licked his hand, then rose up and hopped off the couch. He wagged, then headed to the bathroom, so Rey gave him plenty of privacy. The sounds he heard kinda broke his heart, groans and grunts and heavy panting. Apparently it was easy for Dylan to shift in his sleep, but awake, it must hurt.

That was just awful. Rey could shift with a thought. Really, sometimes he shifted when he didn't want to. He couldn't imagine it hurting.

After the flush, Dylan ran some water, then came back wearing a pair of sweats. That broad chest was bare, and little droplet of water hung, suspended in Dylan's dark chest hair.

Rey licked his lips, his body responding to the sight of all that gorgeous flesh. Oh goddess. Dylan was magnificent.

"Hey. What all do you need out of your car? I really think we need to think twice about going back to it." Dylan settled next to him on the couch, pulling down a folded blanket to cover... both of them. Snuggling.

"Clothes. I have a toiletry bag. Mostly soft clothes." He leaned in, the scent of Dylan surrounding him.

"We'll see what we can do." Dylan put an arm around him, and it seemed so natural, so easy. He just cuddled up. "Mmm. Better."

"Yes." He rubbed his cheek against Dylan's chest, vocalizing softly. Why was this so easy? What was it between them that worked seamlessly?

"Anyway, we'll get you what you need, regardless. What the heck is on the TV?" Dylan sounded very put out that something had overtaken *Top Chef*.

"Uh.... Some housewife monstrosity? Do we have Hulu?"

"We do." Dylan hunted the remote in the cushions, which was a bit like being on a bumpy raft.

Rey began to laugh, the coarse hair on Dylan's chest tickling him.

"Sorry. Sorry." Dylan was laughing too, but they finally found the silly controller.

"You aren't sorry. I can tell." Rey let himself just howl with laughter, his relief, his joy in being alive just bursting out of him.

"I am. Desperately." Dylan snorted, which set them both off again.

He found himself leaning full body against Dylan, not holding himself back in the least. They finally dissolved into a puddle of blankets and chuckled, holding on to one another.

"Oh, that felt good. We needed that, right?" Dylan asked, and Rey had to agree. It had been necessary. "So, *Mummy* movies or *Project Runway* reruns?" Dylan clicked through some of the screens on the TV.

"Brendan Fraiser is kind of hot...."

"Oddly so in those movies, right?" Dylan clicked over to the first in the series.

"Yeah. Him and Oded Fehr are both lovely."

"Oded's not just pretty." Dylan smacked his lips.

"Oh, listen to you! He has all the right things in all the right places, doesn't he?"

"He does." Dylan leaned harder, surprisingly heavy. "Man, I'm just sleepy."

"Rest then." He wasn't going anywhere, was he? No, not now.

"Okay. Stick around in here?" Dylan seemed a little worried he would wander off.

"I'll cuddle in, watch the movie." Rey could make that promise.

"Thank you. You're warm." Dylan nuzzled his cheek, the action pure wolf.

"Thank you." He leaned back with a sigh.

This was so much more pleasant than he'd imagined a safe house to be. Of course, with Mick it would have been a whole different story.

He didn't think Mick liked him very much. At all. In fact, he would go with not at all at all.

Dylan chuckled, but Rey thought he was asleep. Fully.

Weird how Dylan reacted to him even asleep, but cool. He cuddled in and let himself watch Rick and Evie save the world.

The rest would just have to wait until tomorrow.

———

Dylan woke up warm, the world dark and scented of fox. Huh. Neat.

Peering out from under the blanket, he realized it was morning. And he had to piss like crazy.

Rey was curled up in a tight little ball in the center of his fuzzy robe, tail over his nose.

Man, they needed to get it together. He woke up as a wolf, Rey was human. Then vice versa. Probably a good thing. The fox was less likely to inspire morning wood.

Although last night? He'd noticed Rey's more than ample wood. Yum.

It was definitely bad to be interested in a client.

Really bad.

Incredibly deeply bad.

Right. Bathroom. Not gawking. Peeing.

He hit the head, then washed up and went to see what their breakfast situation was. Leftover doughnuts and a Keurig machine with... peppermint mocha cups.

Okay. That was doable. Not particularly manly, but doable.

He made up coffee, then checked cabinets. Lucky Charms and shelf-stable milk. That had to be the bear. Kit did love Lucky Charms. Rice. Lots of rice. What the hell? Oh right. That sweet little panda they'd had to guard from a crazed stalker.

He would go with doughnuts and take them to Denny's later for eggs. Rey needed the stuff from his car anyway, right? Coffee first.

Rey woke up, stretching, turning from fuzzy to human in a single easy motion. Dylan blinked, then smiled as Rey covered up with the blanket.

"Morning."

"Good morning. Doughnut?"

"Coffee?" Sleepy and rumpled fox was adorable. Biteable. *Down, boy.* What the hell was he thinking getting all silly?

"I'm making it now." He filled the water, then popped in a cup.

"You need help?"

"I think I can manage." Maybe. He pressed the Brew button, and sure enough, it worked. He slid a mug under the spout just in time.

Rey applauded for him, and he looked over, but there wasn't a hint of malice, just a happy little grin.

"I know. I'm a dork in the morning. I swear, I'm worse than a bear. And I know one...."

"Yeah? I've never met one, I don't think." Rey looked impressed.

"I'll introduce you. He works at the office."

"Okay. He is sweet?"

"He is. Such a teddy bear. Ta-da! Coffee."

"Oh, peppermint. I love peppermint. Thank you!"

God, he wanted to kiss Rey. Right now. The idea made him suck in a deep breath, wondering what the hell.

"I'm glad you like it." He put in another K cup, needing to keep busy so he kept his hands to himself.

"So how did you get into your line of work?" Rey sipped his coffee, copper eyes focused on him like he was fascinating.

"I was a cop." He didn't elaborate on those years. They hadn't been all bad, but as a wolf, he'd been bombarded with the smell of blood so often.... "When I left the force, I knew Mick already, so I applied to his agency." He'd liked Mick the first time the guy had shown up at the station, needing to talk shop about a suspect. Together they'd formed a pack—unusual and odd, but wonderful.

When he added in the kitties and the bear, well, they had a family like no other. Tight-knit and efficient.

"What about you?" Dylan asked. "How does a guy get into your job?"

"It's what I'm good at. Typing, talking to people online, meeting people, learning things, googling madly. One day someone paid me to research something in college. Then I started doing more and more, and suddenly I had a career."

"So it started out as research assistant? What did you study in college?" Rey was so much more interesting than his old ass.

"Library science," Rey answered promptly.

"That's a thing?"

"It most definitely is."

He eyed Rey to see if he was serious. "Wow. I had no idea. I went to the academy, and I have an associate's in criminal justice."

"That's immensely cool. I love the idea of studying people and their behavior."

"People can be... challenging." He chuckled. "Not as much as crocs." Crocs were stinky, gross, and mean.

"Crocs are.... Gracious. Do you think there are good ones?"

"I hope so?" Maybe not. Maybe when they shifted, the lizard brain just couldn't support human thoughts.

"Me too. They didn't seem... good."

"Nope." Dylan popped a couple of doughnuts each in the microwave for twenty seconds to freshen them. Carrie had taught him that. Their girl hated stale bread stuff.

"Oh, clever! That doesn't melt the icing?" Curious little fox.

"Not just the short time it's in." He placed the warmed

doughnuts on the counter. Apple fritters and maple. The boss did love him.

Then he was sitting next to Rey again, and he swore the scent of Rey was better than the pastry. He wanted to move closer, and he did, scooting his chair over.

Rey's nose worked, scenting him, and Dylan had to admit that made him ache. He didn't need to be springing wood around his clients, but this one inspired him, got to him so fast he had no defense.

He grabbed a fritter, hoping Rey didn't want them both. Raisins. So weird. He liked them as a human, but his wolf thought they were poison.

"You mind if I have one too?" So polite.

"Not at all, honey. I thought you would like one of each too." He beamed when their fingers touched at the plate when he reached for his maple one.

Rey hummed softly. "You're... warm."

"Am I? Is that bad?" His arm pressed against Rey's, and they shared scent, which made him hard as a rock.

"No. No, this is.... Not bad." Rey moaned softly, sliding toward him instead of away, which was probably smarter.

"Not at all. Though if you don't want me to kiss you, you need to tell me now." Rey's lips looked so inviting, and Dylan would bet they tasted good. Like icing.

Rey raised his face, eyes staring into him, gaze burning, the sweet lips offered to him.

Dylan moaned, because he couldn't resist. He should. A thousand reasons why he should crossed his mind in the seconds before their lips met, meshed, opened to each other.

Rey gasped, electricity buzzing between them.

Yeah. Dylan wanted more, so he tilted his head and went searching for more of Rey's flavor. God, that was a sweet fucking addiction. So fast. This was moving so fast, but his brain wasn't talking. His wolf instinct was.

It didn't surprise him at all when Rey climbed into his lap, licking at his bottom lip and exciting the hell out of him. Dylan gripped that firm little ass, tugging them closer together. This was a far better wake-up than coffee from a pod. Rey was solid, rubbing against him with a deliciously firm prick, their scents mingling.

That cock lived up to the promise of what Dylan had seen the night before, and he pushed open Rey's robe. He needed more. He lifted up too, trying to get out of the sweats.

"Come to the sofa. Please. Or the bed. Somewhere with padding where we can explore." Clever fox.

"Bed, then." It was opposite the windows, where the couch was closer to them. He didn't mind being asleep and being ambushed. But getting busy and being attacked? No.

"Bed." Rey stood and held out one hand to him. Okay, that was dear as fuck. The little fox helping him up.

Dylan took the offered touch, then held hands with Rey into the bedroom. The warm press of palms was so intimate, oddly. So heated and wonderful, how his hand swallowed up Rey's.

He untied his sweats with his free hand, laughing as Rey pushed the pants down over his aching cock.

"Eager." It wasn't a complaint. It was just an observation. This was so damn fast, but Rey was right there with him, leaning against him again, so he wasn't imagining how good this was. How right.

They climbed onto the bed, and he dragged one hand down along Rey's side, petting in a long stroke.

Rey wiggled, arching for him, legs spreading.

Oh, he loved that quick response. Dylan could grow to need it, in fact. If he did, he hoped to hell Rey would be on the same page with him. He leaned back a little bit so he could see, so he could watch Rey twist.

He wanted to see Rey ride him, wanted to watch that hot

little hole take him in. He knew they had a way to go before that, but his brain wouldn't shut up about it.

He began to pant, his hand moving to curl around the heavy balls, rolling, careful not to hurt.

"Oh!" Rey rocked into his touch, the soft, surprised O of his mouth calling to Dylan, begging him to kiss it. He bent, tugging that flushed lower lip with his teeth.

Rey's hands slid around his shoulders, and a rush of warmth bubbled up in him, his cock heavy and throbbing with need. He rocked a little, letting Rey feel him move, feel how good they were together. The kiss went on and on, just slick and apple-maple.

One lean leg wrapped around his hip, and they started to rub, to slowly drag their bodies together. The friction made Dylan want to go faster, but he wanted to savor this too. They had time, didn't they?

"Focus." Rey laughed for him, nipping his bottom lip.

"I am. I want us to slow down and feel it." He smiled into those glittering eyes, fascinated by their color.

"I am totally into feeling you. You smell like heaven on earth." Rey nuzzled his jaw, the motion soft, sweet.

"So do you." He licked his way down Rey's neck, then nibbled one collarbone. Rey groaned and lifted his chin, letting Dylan in easily.

"Mmm." He licked, kissed, and bit. Not hard. Just enough so Rey felt it, and when Rey bucked under him, he got the picture.

More. Dylan gave it, making a strong dent with his teeth.

The sharp little bark made his eyes roll back in his head. Dylan did love some biting. Maybe a little smack here and there to heighten the sensation.

He would never have thought this lean fox would be so strong, so present. Rey had seemed so... quiet. So worried. So self-contained.

Here, in this bed, Rey was quick to touch, to share scent and warmth. Maybe it was instinct. Maybe they were both just hungry.

He hoped it was more than that, because it felt fucking right. Here and now it felt as if they were forming the kind of bond he thought he could only have with another wolf. Cosmic.

Cosmic. Listen to him.

Dylan lapped his way down to one hard nipple, needing to explore. When he sucked it in, Rey hummed, the sound so encouraging that he stayed there, worrying the tiny nub.

Rey whimpered softly, and one soft hand slipped down Dylan's belly to circle the tip of his cock, to slide over the slit.

His toes curled, his body lighting up like the Fourth of July. "Oh, honey."

"Yes." Rey touched him like he knew every inch, like he had a map that pointed to each and every sensitive spot. The man just seemed to know, from the spot just under the head of Dylan's cock to the crease of his thigh.... Hell, that was almost better than the cock, ticklish and yet fiery.

Rey lingered there, touching him until he wanted to turn Rey over and drive into him.

Instead, Dylan yanked Rey back up on his lap, kissing that sweet mouth for all it was worth. He thought it was worth a hell of a lot.

Rey wrapped around him—legs and arms—and held on, that flat belly rubbing against him. They were cooking with oil suddenly, both of them panting and moaning, Rey dancing in his lap. "Little minx."

"Fox."

"Right. Not a rodent." He chuckled, then grunted when Rey grabbed his nipple and twisted. "Ow! Okay, not even close."

No, Rey was a fox through and through, no matter what Brock said.

Rey laughed, baring white teeth, before bending to bite where he'd twisted.

"Toothy!" Dylan loved all the little things he was learning about his lover. Rey seemed so shy and retiring but was a voracious lover.

"One good turn, hmm?" Rey's teeth dragged over his skin, nipping just a little hard on the very tip.

"Oh." Damn. His skin was burning right around that nipple, and his cock was so damn interested.

"Mmm-hmm." Rey made his eyes roll. He reached up for Rey's nipple, rolling it in his fingertips as Rey bit again.

They were a circle of pleasure, just testing and teasing, learning each other, and when Rey scooted down, mouth heading toward his cock, Dylan damn near howled.

Instead, he dug his fingers into Rey's thick red hair, holding on. Not pushing. Just encouraging.

Rey focused on the tip, lapping with light, steady touches, dragging against his skin, lighting his nerves. This was a creative, needy lover, and he reveled in watching Rey lick at his skin, that tongue shockingly pink. He promised himself he'd pay the favor back. Afterward.

First he needed to feel this, to let Rey touch him.

He pushed up, letting his hips rock to give Rey more, to ask for more.

"Mmm-hmm." Rey opened up, tongue sliding down along his shaft.

"That's—oh. Oh." Dylan felt like he'd lost words. He'd had more than one blowjob in his life. This felt like— No. No words. None.

Rey cupped his balls and rolled, squeezing him with a gentle, careful hand.

Gritting his teeth, Dylan pushed at Rey's head, wanting

more of that mouth. He needed sucking. Deep sucking. Rey opened up, taking him in a slow, steady, breath-taking swoop.

"Uhn." He fell back on his elbows, still watching, but not wanting to choke Rey with the hold he'd had. Rey took him to the root, lips fastened tight around the base of his cock.

They moved together, Rey bobbing up and down, Dylan rising up with his hips before falling back to the bed. His belly pulled in tight, his skin flushed and hot. Rey sucked him like he was a Popsicle, open on the way down, lips tight on the upswing.

That was all he could bear, and he jerked and danced, curses falling from his mouth. He groaned when Rey tapped his balls again, a little rougher now. "Again, honey. I'll make you fly. Do it again."

Rey dove down and sucked like a Hoover, fingers rolling his balls almost too hard.

"Rey!" He came deep in Rey's throat, that mouth moving on him the whole time, making him nuts. He was.... Oh, God, when had he come like that, ever? Certainly not recently.

Maybe when he'd first started jacking off as a teenager.

He leaned back on his elbows, fighting to breathe, to recover, because he intended to tear Rey up, make him fly.

Soon.

Rey smiled up at him, then reached down to stroke that long, slender cock. "That was hot, Dylan."

"God, yes. Come here, honey. Let me touch you." He grabbed Rey under the arms and tugged.

"Oof." Laughing, Rey sprawled on him, cock against his hip. "Hello."

"Hey. I want to make you feel good too." He slid one hand down to squeeze Rey's asscheek. He bent to take a hard kiss, tasting his own salt on Rey's lips.

That was possibly the most amazing thing ever. He let Rey

hump against him for the length of the kiss, but then he flipped them, stretching Rey out beneath him.

"Mmm...." Oh, he didn't think he'd seen anything so fine since he'd watched Rey suck him off.

Dylan grinned, then bent to suck up a mark just under that collarbone so it would only show to him. No one else would see it. It gave him a jolt, the idea that he and Rey would share this secret.

"Oooh." Rey wiggled beneath him, skin sliding on his, cock even harder every second.

He pressed one thigh between Rey's legs, giving his little fox some pressure, some friction.

"Yes!" Those fingers could dig right in and grab with surprising strength. Rey seemed fascinated with his body hair, tugging at it, carding it with his nails.

The little pulls and stings made him bite, made him nuzzle in and nibble at the curve of Rey's jaw.

Rey kept moving, slipping and sliding, finally settling that cock against his balls, where the hair was wiry, giving more friction. Someone liked a little ache; maybe needed it.

Dylan was happy to give it. He pinched the join of thigh and ass, hopefully not too hard. The moan he got told him he was doing a great job.

"Dylan." His name was bitten out, Rey's teeth snapping together. "More."

"Yeah?" He pinched again, then slapped a little, his hand rebounding off.

"Uhn!" Tendons stood out as Rey arched back, his neck and shoulders tight.

"So damn pretty. Made for me." He really believed that right now, in this moment.

"Please."

He nodded and swatted again, just enough to warm, to get his little fox revved up and ready. No one needed to have purple skin, but Rey growled and slammed against him, and he just... damn. He was gonna rise again, which shocked him to no end.

Rey was inspiring.

Rey pulled one leg up at the knee, exposing himself, baring himself shamelessly, and that left Dylan moaning, his entire body shuddering.

He put two fingers to Rey's mouth. "Get me all wet, honey. I want in you. Got me all hard again. Can we do that? Can I fuck you?"

Rey's answer was a low cry, those fuck-swollen lips wrapping around his fingers, the suction trying to stop his heart.

It didn't, so he let Rey get his skin good and slick before pulling free. He pressed both fingers to that tight, hot little hole, demanding Rey let him in. The tight ring of muscles gripped him, squeezing his fingers like a fist.

"Open up. Come on, Rey. Let me in." He moved in tiny motions until Rey eased up. Then Dylan pushed in deep to get Rey ready.

Rey arched under him, bucking hard on his fingers. When he brushed Rey's gland, a sharp cry sounded, filling the air.

So he did that again too, wanting Rey to overload on sensation just as he had. Dylan pulled free not much later, not wanting to get dry. He let Rey slick his cock up with spit too, before lifting Rey's hips and sliding between those spread legs.

"Tell me you want this." He wasn't going to do anything Rey wasn't into.

"I want you. Fuck me. Hard." Okay, that was clear.

Dylan nodded, the tip of his cock popping through the grip of Rey's tight ring of muscle. After that it was a long, slow glide until his hips sat flush with Rey's ass.

They were hot against his skin, and he knew the wiry brush of his curls had to rasp just so.

Rey nodded, sweat dripping off his face. "Please. Please, Dylan. More. Move."

Now it was his turn to nod, and he pulled back to push forward again. The heat made him flex, his abs pulling hard to drive him in.

Rey bared his teeth, legs wrapping around Dylan's waist, yanking him in. Demanding man. Dylan loved it. He slammed them together, his teeth gritted, his body on fire once more.

"Feel you, Rey. I can feel how hot and tight you are. Want you to come on my cock." He just babbled, loving the way they fit together.

"Please. Please, yes. Don't stop."

Oh, Rey begged so prettily.

"Not going to, honey. Not until we're done." He was rocking and rolling, and this was round two, so he could last.

Rey groaned for him, moaning low and deep as he bucked, squeezing hard.

The tight grip of Rey's body might be the death of him. He could handle that, but he didn't want to leave Rey unsatisfied. He reached down and began to stroke, thumb working the tip.

Those copper eyes flew open wide, Rey flailing for a moment. So cute. Less cute was the way Rey's body gripped his cock, proving how desperate Rey was for those touches. So Dylan stroked up and down, giving every callus on his hand, every bit of his strength. Every upward stroke made Rey gasp, the slit of Rey's cock leaking.

"I want to see you come so bad." Dylan wanted to lick Rey's spunk off his hand.

"Need this." Rey's rough whisper dragged on his nerves.

"Yes. Need you. God, honey. Faster." They needed to move so much quicker.

"Fas... faster. Fuck...." Rey's eyes rolled up in his head.

Dylan rocked up and down, one hand on Rey's hip to

speed him on. There was no way this could go on much longer. They needed release.

Rey shot with a wild cry that echoed inside him, bouncing in the air.

Dylan came a second time, the pleasure a softer wave this time, but no less amazing. Watching Rey gave him such damn joy.

He didn't want to explore that too deeply, the immediate attraction, the pull that the fox had on him. Not now. He wanted to rest and bask in the glow. Then Dylan knew they had to get back to work.

They still had to find out what was going on with Rey and who was after him. A deeply personal relationship would cloud things....

Said the man with his cock buried in Rey's ass.

Yeah, that was about as deep as a man could get.

When Rey bent to kiss him, he gave up thinking. This connection was worth the work complications. The rest of it was just legwork.

FIVE

R ey was sore in the best possible way, aching deep down. It was delicious, arousing, and, to be honest, slightly distracting, given that they had to move along and get things done. He needed to get stuff out of his car, meet the bear in the office, and probably get grilled again by the entire staff. Dylan needed to do... well, all sorts of things, including check-in with the tech guy, from what he understood.

Rey dressed in his newly washed and dried clothes, then waited for Dylan to be ready to go. He didn't want to be a panicky idiot, so he focused on breathing. Deep breaths in and out, which he hoped would help to calm him.

One big hand landed on the back of his neck. "You okay?"

The touch flooded him with a sudden comfort, and he nodded. "I am. I'm ready and able to move on."

"Cool. Now, I want to just go over a few things. We'll have backup at the office, but I still want us in and out of your car as quickly as possible. If I say run, you run. No arguments. Okay?"

"No arguments. I'm not stupid." Neither was he particularly brave.

"Good man." Dylan dropped a quick kiss on his mouth. "Check the window? I'll get the back door, make sure it's safe to go to the car."

"Of course. No crocs." None. Zero. Zip.

"Nope. Or any other predator who stinks and eats turtles...."

He had to laugh at that. Dylan was trying hard to help him stay calm. Rey forced himself to push the curtain away, peek outside. He didn't see anything odd. He sniffed hard.

No weird smells, thank goodness.

"Okay, let's move out." Dylan held out a hand to him.

Their fingers twined together, that increasingly familiar jolt sliding up his arm. Dylan just did it for him, whatever it was. He'd never let someone do what Dylan had done to him so quickly, and never had he engaged in sex quite so wildly.

Pheromones. Pheromones plus stress.

Possibly pheromones plus stress multiplied by hot ex-cop. Dylan was big and shaggy and looked relatively harmless until he took his clothing off.

One way or the other, every time they got close enough to touch, his body got hot, ready.

"I can smell you, honey. Relax." Dylan leaned down and nuzzled his temple. "Breathe."

"Sorry. Sorry, I don't want to get you in trouble."

"With who?" Dylan led him out the back, the same way they'd come in the day before.

"Your people? Your boss? He doesn't like me already." Rey knew that, no question.

"Oh, he just needs to get over himself."

The SUV looked normal, but Dylan checked all around it before letting him in. So cautious.

Dylan put him in the front seat, then went around the

front. No expression of fear or anger appeared. Maybe they were okay.

Dylan crawled into the vehicle, closing the door behind him and locking it. "Let's go. I don't like being out in the open."

"Me either. Will they follow us? I mean from the office. My car is there, so once we show up...."

"We'll take precautions. Don't worry."

"Okay." Certainly. He had nothing at all to worry about. Nothing.

Dylan winked over at him, those eye lines so crinkled and cute. How anyone could think his wolf was cute.... But he did.

"Really, Rey. I'll take care of you."

He leaned up, touched their cheeks together. "I believe you."

"Good." Dylan beamed, then put them in reverse. "So, we'll look at your car, then maybe swing by the HR office where the victim worked."

"My contact hasn't called back, hasn't emailed." The lack of communication made a ball of worry curl into his belly.

"Which is why I think we ought to stop by. You did business with them; it's not like you can't go to their offices for another 'job.'" Dylan made air quotes around job.

"Right. Right, I'll stop in." He wouldn't go into a bathroom where crocs might find water, but he'd see if Corde was there.

"We will." Dylan gave him a cop-like glare.

"Are you going to be my assistant?" As if Dylan could look like anyone's mere assistant.

"I am. I think it will be good to show you have some muscle with you."

Oh, he'd make a show of it, wouldn't he? Dylan was a stone-cold stud, and Rey loved the idea of having the wolf at his side. He clapped his hands with delight.

That way if it was the former PR office after him, well, they would know he had backup.

He leaned his head back against the seat, his throat working as they drove.

"You need something to drink? I can stop."

"No. No, I'm just…." *What? Scared? Worried? Stressed?* "I'm fine."

"I'm so sorry you have to go through this, but I'm not a bit sorry you came to me." Dylan put a hand on his thigh.

The worry, the stress just melted away in a heartbeat. How… fascinating, that a simple touch should make him so pleased.

"Do you feel that, Dylan?"

"Feel how good it is to touch you? Yes."

Rey wasn't sure that was an answer. Maybe it was just him. Maybe he was just that high-strung. Maybe he was just a dork.

No.

Dylan's touch made him melt.

Dylan rubbed a little, derailing his thoughts again. "We'll head to the office, get your things, stow your car, say hi, visit the PR firm, then go have tacos."

"I love tacos! How did you know? Did I tell you?"

"Um. I can't remember if you did or not." Dylan chuckled. "That's good, though. I love tacos so bad."

"Mmm." With pico. He loved pico de gallo. And maybe a side of rice, if it looked right, because rice was truly the craps roll of Mexican food.

"I can imagine watching you eat tacos, honey. I bet you like the crispy ones."

"I do. Wait, watching me? Is that good?"

"Well, not as good as it would be to watch you eat ice cream, but yeah. Good."

Oh. Oh! Goodness.

"I am good at ice cream cones, Dylan. Very. I never miss a drip."

Dylan moaned, and if the sound was a little exaggerated, it was okay. He could feel from the way heat filled the front seat that Dylan would like to see him eat a cone. He licked his lips, picturing it.

"I'll get us ice cream after tacos...." Dylan's voice had gone husky.

"We should take it somewhere private. Somewhere we can... share." Rey was flirting madly, but he was in for a penny, in for a pound now.

"Now that sounds like the best idea I've heard all day, and you're full of good ideas. So am I." The constant teasing distracted him until they were on the interstate and moving fast. That made everything easier. Crocs didn't seem like big interstate drivers.

Maybe that was wishful thinking, but those guys had been all *grrr* and tooth and not much brain.

They pulled off about twenty minutes later, heading in toward Dylan's office. His poor baby car. He hoped it wasn't trashed.

Surely it wouldn't be, right? It was a private detective's parking lot.

They had to know that, whoever they were.

That was the scariest thing about the whole situation, having no idea who was after him. Or why. So he couldn't do anything about it, because he couldn't do research or call about for information.

He could still hear Mick telling Dylan to find out what he was hiding, but there wasn't anything. Should he have given Elise the files? They were hers, weren't they? About her. Nothing earth-shattering.

"You're thinking loud."

"I'm trying to figure out what I did wrong."

"Honey, this isn't you. You didn't do anything, I'd bet on it. Someone else either thought you were a good place to hide something, or it's mistaken identity."

"I haven't been, like... shot with a microchip or anything." Had he? Rey hadn't felt any strange bumps, lumps, or flu-like symptoms, and he was quite sensitive to such things.

"Well, if you have been, James can find out, I guess." Dylan shook his head. "I mean, I doubt it?"

He noticed Dylan wasn't ruling it out.

"You would have noticed last night, right?" He would have in the shower. Except those croc's eyes had hypnotized him....

"I would have. I touched every inch of you, honey. I have a bug scanner, though, if it will make you feel better." Dylan was humoring him, but that was okay. It was sweet.

"Anything to keep me out of suspicion, huh?"

They pulled into the parking lot, his car right there, safe and sound. Not a scratch on it, from the initial view.

In fact. Dylan parked right next to it. "Let me text Kit. He's the bear. He can shift in a heartbeat, so he'll come stand watch." Dylan tugged out his phone.

"Yeah. I think I'll stay right here, though...." Rey tingled like he was wide-awake, like he was buzzed. Crocs didn't move fast in the cool weather, right?

Adrenaline.

"That's fine. You tell me what I'm looking for."

"Huh?" Crocodile? Surely Dylan hadn't forgotten.

"No, in the car. You want to stay here, right?" Dylan frowned, looking confused.

"I meant until you texted. Sorry. I'm.... Does it feel weird out there to you?"

"Not that I can tell yet, but you notice things. What feels weird?" Dylan finished tapping.

"I feel tingly. As if I'm being hunted." Rey cast his gaze about again.

"Okay." Dylan looked in the rearview, eyes moving, never staying too long in one place. That nose moved too. Just the fact that Dylan believed him, trusted in him, made it better.

Someone came into view in his side mirror, but they waved, which bad guys didn't do.

"Okay, that's Kit. Let's do this, honey."

"Right." He forced himself to open the SUV door and grab his keys, then run for the car.

He needed clothes. Work stuff. His mail, which he'd grabbed before going to meet Elise. His box with his papers—passport, etc.

The rest of the stuff was bibs and bobs from the apartment. Keepsakes. His coffee maker.

Those could sit in the car. Maybe he could get Dylan to move it to a storage unit.

The grass moved in the wind, and his heart stopped in his chest.

"Hey. Smell anything, Kit?" Dylan asked the big guy who joined them.

"Fish. Rotten fish."

"Oh fuck," Dylan spat.

Yeah, Rey concurred. Fuck was about right.

"Inside," Dylan barked. "Crocs are here. Now!" Dylan drew his weapon, pushing Rey after Kit. Kit grabbed Rey up and ran, sprinting for the building.

He could really run for a big guy. Rey was getting used to being carried around, for all that he wasn't tiny.

The *pop-pop* of a gun going off made him wince, ducking into Kit's body.

"You're okay." The door flew open and he was tossed, right into Mick's waiting arms.

Kit whirled and ran back out, and a jaguar streaked by him, snarling as it ran.

Mick drew him deep in the building, keeping him away from the windows.

"Just stay down, kiddo. My guys have this." Mick's confidence did help, which surprised him. Perhaps wolves had a way about them that comforted, though Dylan was more his thing.

"I can't believe.... They're so awful." And Dylan was out there with them. *His* Dylan.

"I want to know what the hell they want. Dylan says you're not at fault, and I trust his gut. But I need you to think hard. What else might tie you and the dead lady together? Anything?" Mick waved his hands in the air.

"Just the man I got the file from, and... whoever recommended me to her?" Those were the only two points of contact.

"Okay." Mick paced. "What if it's not her. What else were you working on?"

"I'm gathering information on an Indian CEO for a software company, and I was bidding a job from a fashion designer, but they haven't contacted me yet."

"Have you gotten anything from either of them? Anything someone might have thought you passed on to your HR lady?"

"The fashion designer, no. The software company? Yes, they've sent me a great deal since I'm in the middle of the gathering stage."

"Okay, then we look there." Mick pulled out his phone. "James, I need eyes. What the hell is going on out there?"

"They're coming in. Four dire crocs, boss. Four."

"Coming in? What's the status on Kit and Dylan and Brock?"

The door opened and the guys tumbled in, the scent of dead fish everywhere.

Rey ran for Dylan, heedless of the mess, the smell. "Are you hurt?"

"I'm all right. We need to set up defenses. They're still busting through walls."

"Okay. What can I do?" Rey grabbed his phone even as he asked the question. He could do what he was good at. Research. He typed quickly. "Go for the eyes and the palatal valve in the back of the throat. They can't go fast for any length of time. Too much lactic acid buildup."

"Got it. Hold 'em off. Lots of sirens are on their way." That was James on Mick's speaker.

"They're not going to keep attacking. They'll back off. They're not smart enough to be fiercely loyal." Rey's fingers flew, information popping up on his phone rapidly.

"Then we hold them off. Do we have weapons in here, Brock?" Mick barked. The big boss could snarl.

Brock, whoever he was, snorted. "We have weapons in the breakroom."

"They're backing off, boss. Running into the grasses. Local police are on property." The voice on the radio was calm.

Rey wasn't sure where this James was, but he was obviously watching.

He thought Dylan had said James was the tech guy, so that made sense. His heart was pounding, and everything felt bad and wrong except Dylan against him.

Goddess, what if Dylan was hurt, what if the others were? It would be his fault.

"You're shaking, honey." Dylan held him, half carrying him to a seat.

"Are you okay? I didn't mean to desert you. I just...." He hadn't thought. He'd done what he was told.

"No, I told you to go when I said. You did." Dylan stroked

his back. "It was easier because I didn't have to worry where you were."

"Take Rey upstairs, Dylan. We don't need him questioned when the cops get here. Kit and I will deal with the locals. Carrie is out until next Monday, so I'll put my nice face on." Mick snapped out orders like he never doubted once that everyone would obey.

"You got it, boss. Carrie's okay?" Dylan asked.

"Yeah." Mick pulled a face. "Her mom fell."

"Shit, I'll send a card. Come on, honey. My office." Dylan took him out of the back room they were in. "We can curl up."

He hadn't done anything, had he? Rey thought he was doing basic information gathering. Public records, public domain—things that were accessible.

"You didn't do a thing. The boss just hates to have to call in local LEOs."

"LEOs? I—" Wait. Was his worry that clear, that obvious that Dylan could read it on his face? Rey prided himself on being self-contained.

"Law enforcement officers." Dylan hugged him once they got to the office. "Peanut butter cup?"

"Uhn." He didn't pounce, but honestly, when did peanut butter not make it better?

"Do you like Raisinettes? I can get some at the store."

"I do, yes. Oh, I never expected anyone to try to hurt any of you. I didn't know what else to do when I hired you."

"Stop. We know the dangers. We just didn't think you needed that much security based on your initial information. Now we know." Dylan's tone brooked little argument.

"Yeah." Now they knew he was crazy scared and hunted by big bad ugly lizards.

"No one would believe now that you were doing this to yourself."

"No. No, I wouldn't even begin to know how to arrange this." That was a comfort, he supposed.

"I know." They shared a pair of peanut butter cups, Dylan licking his fingers, then Rey's. Silly wolf, using that amazing tongue of his at an inappropriate moment.

"What do we do now?" Rey leaned in. "Just wait?"

"The boss will want to meet after he and Brock handle the fallout. I fired a couple of warning shots, so they'll have to prove a threat and smooth some feathers."

Rey nodded and drew his legs up, resting his chin on his knees. What a mess. "So, who is Brock?"

"The jaguar shifter. Pretty and sleek in cat form, grumpy and kinda a slob in human form. We'll get through this, you know." Dylan kissed the top of his head. "Rest up. Adrenaline is hell."

"I just feel like a bad luck charm." One that drew scary crocodiles.

"You have an amazing sense of danger." Dylan chuckled. "We could use a guy like you on the team."

"Me? You all are so... studly." Dylan especially. Rey kept looking, gaze drawn to the strong body, the heavy muscles. Such situations really did heighten things like sexual attraction, which he already felt toward Dylan far out of proportion to how long they'd known one another.

"We need all kinds of skill, honey." Dylan flexed a little, though, didn't he?

"I could lick you all over." The words slid out of him. Stress. It had to be stress, and if he were honest, this mate-like pull he felt toward Dylan.

"Okay. Let me lock the door." Dylan didn't even pretend to argue.

Oh, goodness gracious. Were they genuinely going to do this now, with crocs and police downstairs? He put his legs down to make room for his cock. It was growing rapidly, especially since Dylan was kinda stripping right off.

Dylan walked straight up to him, and his lips parted like someone had pushed a blowjob button.

This was the craziest thing he'd ever done, and recently he'd had two brushes with crocodilian death. Still, how often did a beautiful man offer him his cock?

He rather hoped Dylan would do it a lot. Right now was good, though. He dragged his tongue over Dylan's slit, gathering up the salty goodness. He'd discovered a real talent for sucking Dylan last night.

"Mmm. Oh, Rey." Dylan's moan was low in pitch, but heavy in intensity. "I.... Don't stop, sweet one. I ache for you."

There was no way he would stop now, but the praise felt amazing.

He hummed, wanting to add vibration, to let Dylan know how happy he was. Dylan went up on tiptoe, rocking in a slow roll. Someone liked that. A lot.

Dylan slid one hand over the back of his head, cupping it, drawing him down on that heavy cock.

Rey closed his eyes, letting Dylan guide him. This was pure pleasure for both of them. Soft words poured down on him, praise and need, and it made him dizzy. Those hard fingers were so gentle in his hair, asking instead of demanding. It was the strangest thing—this weird peace in a maelstrom of insanity. He needed it so bad, and he would get what he could.

Dylan did that. Rey had taken lovers before, but none of them could calm him with a touch. He really felt as if they were meant to be together, a hope he tamped down on as soon as he felt it. This was just stress, but he would take it.

"Yeah, we're good here, safe. I swear."

He nodded slightly. Not enough that his teeth dug in or anything, but enough that Dylan would feel him, know he was listening.

"Sweet. Oh, Rey, that's sweet. More." Dylan was rumbling, almost growling. The fine tension he could feel in Dylan's thighs told him he wasn't the only one affected by the tense situation they'd had.

More. He groaned softly and nibbled, teeth barely dragging on Dylan's flesh.

Dylan moaned far louder, starting to move faster and fuck his lips, pressing into him with need. They rocked together, Rey gripping Dylan by the hips, opening wide so that Dylan could take him, hold him. He would mourn the loss of that flavor. Of Dylan's scent.

"Just focus on right now, honey. I have this. You."

"Mmm." Dylan could have anything he wanted. Anything at all.

He took Dylan down to the root and began to swallow, over and over, one hand cupping the soft balls.

Dylan did growl then, the scent of musk intensifying. Dylan came for him, hot stuff sliding down his throat, and he took it. Every drop. He cleaned Dylan's sensitive cock, tongue lashing the shaft.

"Fuck." Dylan pulled away, then dropped to the floor on his knees. "Now you, honey."

He gasped, surprised. Why he hadn't thought that Dylan would touch, he didn't know. He'd been totally focused on his wolf, on creating pleasure to get past the fear he'd felt.

Dylan chuckled, opening Rey's clothes, tugging out his cock. "Want this."

"Yours. I mean, you can have me."

Dylan looked up, meeting his eyes with that green gaze, which held only intense desire. No surprise or hesitation. "Mine."

Rey nodded, caught in Dylan's look.

Dylan stroked him, hand working him slowly, the pattern mesmerizing. Yes, he was Dylan's, lock, stock, and barrel.

"That's right, Rey. Every inch."

"Yes." He breathed hard, his lips parted. God, watching that made him even harder.

Dylan curled the fingers of his free hand, tapping his hole, teasing him.

His toes drew up, his belly pulling in. "Harder."

"Yes." The tapping became a tiny sting.

He caught his breath, his eyes wide. Oh heavens.

Dylan chuckled softly and shook his head, murmuring, "You're beautiful."

"I—am I? Thank you." He had no idea what he was right now. Just a ball of need. Oh, such need. His body felt tight, hot, his balls heavy.

Dylan began to stroke him, faster, harder, the touches making his heart flutter. He dug his heels into the floor beneath the cot, his whole self straining to get more of Dylan's touch.

"Good. Good man." Dylan stared down at his cock, his own hand.

"I—please. Dylan, please. I need." Asscheeks clenching, he panted, his chest heaving.

"Come for me, sweetheart. Let me have it."

"I—oh yes." *Sweetheart.* Such a lovely combination of words, one no one had ever said to him before. Rey shot, his come spreading over Dylan's hand. He shook with the sensations, his balls aching, his heart racing violently.

Dylan eased his touch, relaxing his hand, which was utterly necessary because his prick immediately became sensitive as hell. He needed to come down a little, to rest. Everything was such a whirlwind.

"Shh, honey. Breathe. Rest."

"But...."

"We're going to just hang out up here until the locals leave." Dylan carefully cleaned him off, then tucked him back into his pants. Dylan rose, only to pull on sweats and a T-shirt, then join him on the cot. "Let me hold you, huh?"

"Please." He didn't understand what was happening between them, how this connection happened. He'd heard of wolves mating for life and such, but never once had he heard of a fox and wolf doing the same thing. Maybe, if he were very lucky....

He wasn't sure he could understand, but he knew Dylan was quickly becoming the most important thing in his life.

"Shhh. Do all foxes think as much as you do?"

"I think so, yes. That's why I'm good at—" He yawned and stretched. "—at what I do."

"Ah. I'm just well-trained."

"Mmm. Wolves are pack animals. You read body language and facial expressions better than any other mammal save primates. So you have both." He patted Dylan's chest.

"My smart little mate," Dylan whispered.

"Hmm?" Rey blinked slowly, steadily, the soothing touches sending him down into his dreams, where the word *mate* was the best thing ever.

Six

Dylan lay staring at the ceiling, hardly able to believe what he'd just said.

It was true, though. So true. Rey was his mate. Just.... Wow.

Mick was going to kill him.

Not only because of the whole "It's been less than twenty-four hours" thing, but because of the whole "Good Lord, he's a client" thing.

And a fox.

Dylan always figured he had two strikes against him finding a mate. He was gay, and he was a gay wolf. The pack had to accept anyone he would find, and back when he'd been a rookie cop, those strikes kept him from even looking for anyone.

Luckily, his pack these days had a bear, two cats, and a Mick.

He watched Rey rest, the dark auburn hair just barely tipped with white. The man's features were sharp—nose and chin, cheekbones.

So lovely.

All he could do was smile and stroke Rey's hair until the knock came at his office door.

He rolled away, padded to the outer office, and let in Mick.

"Hey, boss. How'd it go?" Mick didn't look murderous, so it had to have gone okay with the crocs as well as the cops.

"They got away."

"Shit. I mean, what else was gonna happen. No one wants to take on a croc." Not even him. Those things scared the fuck out of him.

"This room smells like sex, Dylan." Mick stared at him, then at the back office.

"Yep." He, in turn, stared Mick down, willing him to drop it.

"Huh. We're going to have a long talk once this job is done, buddy."

Of that he had no doubt, but he could take what Mick dished out. The guy had a lot of bluster, but he cared.

"Got it. Look, I have no idea—"

Mick cut him off. "Rey was telling me there was a business guy. High mucky-muck from India."

"India? Who?"

"Ask your guy," Mick snapped.

"He's sleeping."

"Goddamn it, Dylan—"

"Look, we can all sit and hash this shit out together. James can do on the moment research. But we need rest, and we need to figure out how to keep Rey safe. Okay?"

"How the fuck did the crocs find him? They weren't at the safe house, right?" Mick crossed his arms over his chest.

"No. His car is here, though. I think they were playing averages. Does James have eyes on the car?"

"He does. He snuck it in when the cops were distracting everyone, including anyone who might be watching." Mick looked utterly satisfied by that. "I did a good thing, hiring the kitty."

"About that."

"We'll see about the fox, man. Are you hungry?" Mick's dark eyes flashed with deep want for food.

"Oh my God, starving."

"Come on. Burgers downstairs." Mick opened the door, pointing out with his chin.

"I need shoes." Dylan headed back to his mate, not wanting Rey to freak out waking up alone. "Honey, I'm going downstairs to get some food. Do you want anything?"

Rey murmured something unintelligible, then curled up, gone soft and fuzzy.

Okay. He kissed his nose, then headed back out to Mick. "Burgers."

"Burgers." He went down with Mick, his belly growling loud enough to hear. It was all the sex, all the shifting, all the damn crocs were enough to make him feel like he was starving.

All the time.

Mick hadn't had sex, he reckoned, but the adrenaline was real. Kit was probably eating the whole office.

"Is your fox okay? I grabbed him pretty hard." Speaking of Kit, the question was soft, worried, their bear so gentle.

"He's small." Dylan winked. "He's worn out. Sleeping. But he's okay."

"Crocs." Brock spat out the word, his grumpy kitty face on in full force. "What the fuck?"

"Right? Who did he piss off?" James shook his blond head. "Those things move fast."

"He was saying something about an Indian businessman. Bad business practices." Mick was stuck on that, repeating it to all and sundry.

"Yeah?" James perked up from his boneless kitty slump in the corner. "I might could dig something up on that angle."

"I bet you could. We just need to know who," Mick grumbled. "Dylan won't ask."

"Well, he's asleep." Dylan snapped it out, and all his guys looked right at him, eyebrows raised.

It was Kit that started sniffing, big head tilting.

"Stop it." Dylan glared at Kit, who raised both hands in a clear gesture of surrender.

"Right. Nose off." Kit's smile never turned the least bit mocking.

"Thank you. All of you keep your noses to yourselves." The last thing he needed was his colleagues all weighing in on his thing with Rey.

He and Rey needed to figure out what exactly was going on first. Then he might entertain the guys' remarks. But probably not.

"He's a client, Dylan. That's all I'll say." Mick gave him an impartial glare.

"I know. I'm not sorry." He wasn't about to apologize for his mate. No way.

Rey was everything to him already. Such a short time, but he knew for sure he would protect Rey with every ounce of strength in him. Even from his team, his pack.

"Okay, as long as we're all clear." Mick's answer surprised him.

Brock's "Really, Wolfy? A fox?" didn't.

"I'm not sure what you have against foxes," Dylan said. "But leave mine out of it."

"Yours. *Meu Deus.*" Brock rolled his eyes. "Okay, well, we're kind of at a dead end until you let us talk to him."

"I doubt it. James?"

"Huh?" James started, then shook his head. "Well, no facial recognition on the crocs. I mean, no one expected there to be, right? Dire crocs are few and far between, though, so I did some searching. There was a murder two months ago. The one eyewitness swore the killer was a crocodile. Cops were plain old humans and didn't buy it. They thought their witness was on drugs."

Hell, Dylan would bet the witness thought he was on drugs too.

James's faint grin said he was thinking the same thing. "Anyway," James went on, "the best I can do is follow the po-po investigation, but you guys know how productive that is.

"He told me some info on his other jobs—something about a software company being bought out by a company in India."

"Are you talking about WiseEyes?" James perked up. "You didn't say that before. You just said Indian CEO."

"I just remembered. And he didn't give me any names." Dylan spread his hands, knowing getting defensive did him no good.

"Yeah, but that one was a big deal." James pursed his lips, that brain just working almost visibly. Sometimes James was like the computers he loved so much. "I'm surprised that someone low-level would get that job."

"Maybe that was the point," Mick said. "Someone thought Rey could fly under the radar?"

"Yeah." James tapped his fingers on the table as if he was typing. "Man, let me do a little research, but... this may be bigger than we thought."

"Shit." Mick waggled a brow. "It feels pretty big now. Where's my burgers?"

Dylan grinned. Food was their way of coming together.

"We're all secure in here," Kit said with a shudder. "They can't get in, right?" Their bear was so sensitive to smell, the crocs had really gotten to him.

"Not now, no. We're locked down, *certo*." Brock said it with such surety that no one questioned him. The guy was former black ops. They all trusted his judgment.

"Good. We'll just stick together, get to the bottom of this." Dylan nodded sharply.

"Yep." Kit started handing out burgers. "Mmm."

They all fell on the food—this was comfort, safety, abundance that soothed the frightened animal inside. They were all apex predators, but a croc could tear them apart and they all knew it.

A bask of them? They had no chance whatsoever.

Maybe if they had a hippo shifter....

Dylan began to laugh, the sound rusty even to him.

Mick looked over to him. "Maybe for Christmas?"

He always thought Mick was a little psychic, knowing what Dylan was thinking with no hint of any kind of mate bond at all. "Yeah. Maybe."

"*Quê?*" Brock scowled. "Stop it. I'm trying to eat. No wolfpack in-jokes."

"I like hippos. Can I have a burger, please? I'll pitch in." Rey stood in the doorway to the lounge, hair standing up in copper tufts.

Dylan smiled at Rey, who was a little blinky but smiling back at him.

"Sure, man. Come on and sit." Kit waved Rey to a chair, then assembled another burger. "You get some rest? That adrenaline rush is killer."

"Yes. Thank you. I was disconcerted, I guess." Disconcerted and well-loved.

"Uh-huh." Brock curled his upper lip.

"Don't make me beat you, kitty," Mick said. "Be nice."

Brock batted his long black lashes. "But it's been so long, *patrão.*"

Rey looked between them, snorted. "Promises, promises."

"Oh ho!" James slapped the table. "He does have teeth."

Rey snapped his teeth together like he had at Dylan early on. "People are often surprised."

Dylan reached for Rey, wanting to make sure he wasn't worried. As soon as he touched, he felt the waves of amusement coming off his lover.

He gasped, his eyes crossing. Was this real? This... connection? Damn. Could he really feel that, or was it wishful thinking?

"Hey, earth to Dylan. Here's your burger." Kit handed him a plate.

"Thanks. We can share, Rey. Then get another one."

"Someone else will have to take a turn cooking," Kit said. "Soon."

"Do you cook, Rey?" Dylan asked. He was curious to know everything about Rey. Every weird fact.

"I do okay. I can follow a recipe."

"Cool." Kit grinned. "You can man the pan after you eat."

"Kit!" Dylan glared.

"What? If you can cross the client line...." Kit winked at Rey, though, inviting him to share the joke, so Dylan didn't snarl.

"At this point we're all targets, and I'm so sorry." Rey pulled in, hands in his lap, shoulders rounded.

"Bah." Mick waved a hand. "Most excitement we've had since that gazelle was being hunted by the African lion. Remember that, guys? Very Disney villain."

"Ah yes. There was much chewing of the scenery." Kit laughed softly. "I got to work that one."

"You did great, kiddo." Mick grabbed Kit for a hug, then took a burger. "Let me eat, and I'll cook the next round."

"Thanks, boss." The look Kit gave Mick was pure hero worship, and Dylan felt a pang for the guy. Mick was so oblivious sometimes, seeing Kit only as a kid brother.

Rey looked between the two, and Dylan felt the curiosity, the wicked little buzz of wonder.

He winked, and Rey ducked his head, chuckling.

"*Deus*, does everyone have ESP but me?" Brock snarled, and for a moment his jaguar face was transposed over his human one. "I'm going to my office."

Rey looked at Brock, then beamed over. "God, you're lovely."

Brock blinked, his human face evincing shock. "Uh. Thanks."

"Combat makes Brock grumpy," Kit said.

"Everything makes Brock grumpy," James countered. "Stay and eat, dummy. We love you too."

"Shut up, pussy cat." Brock sat, though, and Dylan thought their resident grumpy cat looked pleased.

Silly man. They were a team. Brock was just—well, he was having a long dry spell.

A long dry spell and a bad experience.

When one of their own got hurt, none of them forgot it.

Rey hummed, a weird, foxy little sound, before getting up to give Brock a hug. The expression on Brock's face was just like a cat that had been picked up and hugged tight.

Okay, that was adorable. Possibly the cutest thing ever.

"It's okay," Rey said. "I should make fries. Do you like fries, Brock? Are there potatoes, Kit?" Rey had typed up a recipe on his phone. So quick to do things no one noticed.

"Always. I love fries. Make bunches." Kit flipped more meat patties.

"I will!" Rey pulled out the potatoes Kit showed him, then sliced them with the slotted chopper thing Mick had bought just for fries. They were all about the salty potato. All of them, no matter what breed.

Dylan leaned back, then tried for casual. "Rey, you know the job you were talking about, the software company? What did they want?"

"There's a man trying to buy them out. Daksh Patel. Wise-Eyes wanted information on him—they wanted dirt."

"Did you come up with anything?" Mick took his lead, kept the tone easy.

"Not really. I mean, I'm not a private detective like you guys. I deal in information you can mine off the net, from people that want to talk. He's not a very nice man. Lots of rumors sliding on the web about how he does sketchy business, destroys little companies for fun." Rey was concentrating on potatoes, the words offered easily.

"So, did you contact anyone who might have proof?" That was James.

"Yes. A young man named Victor Mills. He had a file on Patel, but I never received it." Rey looked up from his potatoes. "At least, not yet."

"Where do you get your mail?" That was Brock, leaning back so he could see Rey.

"A locked box at my apartment. I have some in my car. There was a lot that day and I just shoved it in."

"Brock?" Mick looked at their resident badass, the request clear.

"On it, *patrão*. Be right back."

"Be careful. They might be out there," Rey cautioned.

"I know." Brock was up and out before anyone could say anything else. The man would get the job done.

"Wow. He's... intense. I like him." Rey headed to the pot Kit had heated for him.

Dylan grinned at Rey. His mate had a generous heart. "He's a good man. He's just...."

"Complex." All of them said it at once.

"Right on." Rey started frying.

"God, that smells good." Kit's nose worked like crazy.

"I have to fry them twice, it says. It'll be a few minutes."

"That's okay. Mick is about to make burgers so I can start eating." Kit had loaded a burger or two on a plate.

"Trade off!" Mick stood, taking the spatula from Kit.

It was fascinating, to watch his team and his fox work together, move around each other like they were dancing. Rey fit right in.

Dylan had to wonder academically if that was because Rey was his mate, or if Rey was just.... Rey.

Brock was back with a handful of mail and some clothes. "I put two loads of your stuff down in the office. I wasn't sure if you needed it."

"Oh, thank you!" Rey just smiled like sunrise.

"Thanks, Brock. So, what have you got?" Dylan asked.

"Bills, bills, junk mail, package from ThinkGeek, postcard from a Bobby in Hawaii. Two packages and a box of... tea?"

"Catnip. It was a gift."

"Catnip?" James peered at the box, eyes wide. "Ooooh."

"You're welcome to it. There are four packets."

"Oh." James looked at Brock. Brock looked at James. They set the catnip aside on the counter.

"So, do we open your mail, Rey?" Dylan asked.

"There's nothing scary in there. Go ahead." Oh, that easy agreement made him want to bounce with pride. Rey had nothing to hide from them.

"Okay, so, James, log this, huh?" Mick grabbed the Think-Geek box.

"On it."

Kit did bounce, which was hilarious on such a big guy. "I love ThinkGeek. Love it."

"So, we have a ThinkGeek box with... a Doctor Who Tardis teapot." Brock set the package aside.

"And matching teacup?" Kit was bouncing harder. Such a nerd.

"Oh, do you have them too?" Rey asked.

"Yes! Oh my God!"

Dylan shared a long-suffering look with Mick.

"Really? A Whovian?" Mick muttered.

"Man, you just said 'Whovian.' You lose all cred." Dylan shook his head sorrowfully.

"What?" Mick chuckled. "Okay, so I like Doctor Nine."

"Ten is best," Kit and Rey said together.

Oh, those two were going to be fast friends, Dylan could tell.

"Second package—pens and a packet of white buttons?" Brock's brow furrowed.

"Yes. I go through a lot of both."

"Why the buttons?" Dylan asked, that curiosity about Rey raising its head again.

"I shift, a lot, and my fox chews off shirt buttons to decorate the den. I can't help myself." Rey gave him a wry smile.

Oh God. That was hysterical. Dylan loved it. He winked. "My wolf likes shoes. Usually Brock's, since they're so fancy."

Brock growled, the sound very much a jaguar cough. "Canids."

"Oh, like you aren't the world's biggest laser light whore." James rolled his eyes.

"What's your weakness, James?" Rey asked.

Kit laughed. "Catnip, so beware."

"Well, you are welcome to mine, like I said. What's in the other box?"

James opened this one up. "A SIM card wrapped up in about thirty thousand pounds of bubble wrap."

Everyone stopped, staring. "SIM card," Dylan repeated. "Did you buy one?"

Rey shook his head, pulling fries out of the fryer so they didn't burn, maybe. "No. Why would I? Mine works perfectly well."

"Is there a receipt?" Mick asked. "A note?"

"Just a postmark from here. Postmarked five days ago." James shook the box.

Rey blinked over his shoulder. "Is there a place to put it in a phone so we might see what's on it?"

"I have a SIM card reader upstairs," James said.

"Of course you do." Kit rolled his eyes. "Fries first?" He looked so hopeful, his nose twitching again. Even as a human, that big nose gave away everything.

"The crocs can wait ten minutes," Brock agreed with a fond smile.

"Maybe even twenty," Mick murmured.

"Oh good. I would hate to have fried these for nothing." Rey set a bowl of fries on the table. They were golden and gorgeous and smelled like heaven.

"Oh Lord, for this potato-cooking fox may we be truly thankful," Mick intoned.

"Amen," they all replied.

SEVEN

The SIM card was from a number Rey didn't know, but the texts they found on it were odd and enlightening.

<he's going to kill me>

<I don't know how to get out of here>

<he's sending his men>

He blinked at the screen James had pulled up. "Gracious. I think my contact sent this. About Patel? I need— How do I find out if Victor is still alive?"

"What was the last name?" James asked, reaching for another laptop, rather amazing in tech mode, all signs of lazy cat gone.

"Mills."

Rey grabbed his phone and started doing his magic too. Surely together they could figure this out.

"Uh, is this him?" James showed Rey a small article in what looked like a local newspaper.

He squinted and nodded. "Yes. Here he is on his Instagram, so they're the same."

"Crap." Mick blew out a breath. "He's dead, kiddo."

"Oh." Rey sat hard. Everyone was dying around him. He should get in his car and drive away. The hamburger and fries sat like lead in his belly, because this was all his fault.

"Rey? You can't run off." Dylan took his hand. "Promise me you won't run off."

He squeezed Dylan's fingers, but they both knew what he needed to do. He couldn't stay here. Oh, he didn't want to leave Dylan at all.

"Rey. Stop and think." That was Mick. "Why did they think you would take this to a PR firm?"

"I don't know. I didn't even know they were sending something to me." So... what was the connection? Where did the lines of information cross between his clients and Patel and all this?

"Right. No running off in all directions without more information. Any of us." Mick spoke as if his word was law.

"See, Rey? Us. You're not alone. Not anymore."

He looked at Kit, who was so sweet to say that. Dylan smiled, nodded, encouraging him.

"Come on, Rey. Help me do this." James poked him, hard. "We don't have time for bullshit. I want to figure this out."

"Ow!" He sighed. "What do you need?" Rey hated the idea of leaving these guys, and who was to say the crocs wouldn't keep coming after them if he was gone? So he would stay.

"Let's figure out whose phone this is, first. What number do you have for your contact?"

Rey tugged out his phone and called up Victor. "Here. See. Not the same."

"Okay, so burn phone? Another person? Other options?" James rattled off stuff.

"Downloaded info onto a random SIM card? Duped info?" Rey shot back.

Brock snorted. "Too much information for a burn phone. Contacts?"

"All jumbled info," James muttered, so Rey suggested looking for image files.

"Good one." James tapped away at his keyboard like a mad musician. "Nothing weird except this one. It's too big."

"Can you extract it and copy it? I'd hate to ruin it."

"Yeah. I can pull it over here. Quarantine it to make sure it won't blow up, then... *boom*." James opened the file.

It was a movie file of a wild-looking man with white hair, tipped with bright red. He roared and stomped, and a half dozen dire crocs moved around him. The soundtrack was horked, but he could hear "kill" and "for me" and "hurry."

Damn.

"Jesus." Mick shook his head, his eyes wide as he watched. "Those crocs are some crazy shit."

"So, that's Patel and—" Dylan cut off, gasping.

The man onscreen shifted.

Tiger.

Goodness gracious.

Rey had never actually seen a tiger shifter. Honestly, James and Brock were his first nontheoretical cat shifters. Well, except his business contact Louis, who was a Manx. He liked Louis. Which meant he should never contact the guy again; he might get him killed.

He was going to live inside a bubble. A big croc- and tiger-proof bubble in the wilds of Canada, or perhaps Borneo.

"Hey." Dylan pulled him closer, and before he knew it, he was in Dylan's lap. "You didn't get anyone killed."

"Elise, at the very least, Dylan. They obviously thought I took her the SIM card. What they thought she would do with it...."

"But you didn't." Dylan stroked his spine, up and down, nice and easy. Easing him.

"No, but—"

"You were doing your job." Dylan sighed. "Look, I snoop for a living. All those crocs had to do was bust into your mailbox or something. Those guys get off on killing."

He looked at his Dylan and chuckled, because the logic of that statement was inescapable. "Okay, that was pretty good."

"Thank you. I mean it."

"Should we give you two alone time?" Brock asked, dark eyebrows gyrating.

"Shut up, butthead. I'm going for sensitive." Dylan stuck out his tongue, the move so young and incongruous with Dylan's serious demeanor.

"*Realmente?* I thought you were going for making the rest of us uncomfortable."

Rey gave Brock as threatening a look as he could. "Hush, or I'll hug you again. So what do we do?"

They all exchanged glances.

Mick was the one to clear his throat. "Well, I guess we need to get all the info we can on this tiger. The only way we're gonna beat him is to kinda do it at his own game."

"Violence?" Rey didn't think he could do that. And where would they find a crocodile not in Patel's service, anyway?

"No. Blackmail. Lure him out in the open. Let him know we have proof he's hurt people. Get him to make another mistake." Mick crossed his arms over his chest.

"Yeah, lure him out in the open, but I don't know where the open is," James muttered.

"I guess that's where I step in. Let me see the video and do some research." Rey smiled. "That's my job."

"Okay. We'll move to my office," Dylan put in.

Mick nodded. "James, get everything you can. Brock, make sure we're secure and armed. Kit, you and I will do some paperwork and maybe go out and go over Rey's car again."

"You got it, boss." Kit beamed over at Rey. "We'll make supper together tonight, huh?"

"We will." Mick gave Kit this look, and Rey wanted to smile. They clearly had a great fondness for each other. Rey wondered if the others saw it or what it meant. Perhaps it was just familial.

"Come on, foxy. Let's get to work." Dylan lifted him up, then stood, taking his hand.

"Foxy? Seriously?" He liked it, though, he had to admit.

"My foxy lover," Dylan said, pitching that rough voice low. "I think it suits."

"Do you?" He shivered hard, his hair standing up on his head.

"I do." Dylan ran that free hand over his ass. "You make me a little crazy, Rey. I know we have work to do, but I want you all the time. I ache for you a bit."

"Just a bit?" He pressed back into the touches.

"Well, give me a chance and I'll get good and revved up again. We need to get work done, though, or we'll never live it down."

Rey sobered a bit. "I don't want anyone else to get hurt."

"I know, honey. It just—we never know how things will work out, you know that, right?" Dylan sounded very cautious. Very private detective.

"I know, but you aren't used to crocs, I know that."

That had his wolf barking out a very real laugh. "No, that's true. We've had some amazing predators. Some freaking awful humans too. These are our first crocs. First tiger as well. He sounded like that one in the *Jungle Book* cartoon movie, kinda."

"Exactly! It's a little creepy and a tiny bit cool."

"Yeah. Are you sure you want to watch this whole video, sweetheart? It might not be pleasant." Dylan was still touching him, little contacts that never stopped.

"No, but someone wants to kill me because it was mailed to me. I guess I have to."

"That's reasonable."

He let out the breath he was holding. Rey had worried that Dylan would fight him on this. That video was meant for him, so he would find something there. He was the only one here who would know even a bit what he was looking for, and he felt relatively baffled.

"Can you please stay with me?" God, was that honestly the weakest thing ever?

"I intend to." Dylan pulled up the file after plugging in the card reader to his laptop. "Okay, pulled up a chair, sweetheart. We'll look at this thing." Dylan tugged out a new legal pad.

Rey thought that was so cute and analog, the way Dylan wrote down every detail in his neat block printing.

He sighed and started the video, looking for clues. Where was it shot? Above ground? Underground? He tried to make believe it was just a movie. Just make believe. That was the only way he was going to get through this.

"I'm right here, Rey. I will protect you." Dylan stroked his arm.

"I'm fine. I'm no bunny." Though what they'd done to the bunny and everyone else he knew didn't bear thinking about.

"I know." Dylan finally rested a hand on his leg. "That doesn't mean you don't need me."

That made him smile. The expression slid away when the sound started, the crocs circling around as if this was some sort of ritual.

He frowned. Okay, they were in a... pool area? A fountain?

Something with a lot of water, but tile... not a hot tub. "What does that look like to you?"

"A pool. Like an old Hollywood kind." Dylan scribbled notes.

"Okay. They have to be local, right? And rare?" Real estate with a marble pool and a fountain. *Come on, Google-Fu, and work for me.*

Even if the property wasn't up for sale now, sites like Zillow kept a record of everything that had been up on it. Or not, even. Okay, there were a few mansions and a couple of McMansions. He paused the playback on the scene with the tiled water feature so he could compare.

"You're amazing, mate," Dylan whispered.

"Hush, you." Oh, that praise felt good, perhaps even heated. This was what he excelled at. Patterns. Stuff matching up. He clicked through pictures, finding pay dirt on an estate in the old fancy district not far from the zoo, where stately homes lined a divided, wide street.

"Look!" He pointed, and Dylan squinted at the picture onscreen.

"Huh. Okay, well, that's good work."

"Thanks. So let's find out who owns this place now. I bet it's a corporate holding, hmm?" Rey tapped at the county deeds and ownership site.

"That's a sucker bet, baby."

"Still, if I can link it to Patel somehow. I can backtrack...." He trailed off, scowling at the site, which might be beyond his capabilities.

"If you can't, James can."

"He's kind of a whiz." Rey's fingers flew over the keyboard.

"So are you. I'm impressed. I want you with me."

"Huh? I am with you."

Dylan laughed, patting his leg. "I mean full-time."

He stopped to stare, their noses meeting when he turned his head.

"Full-time?" Rey blinked. "Seriously."

"Seriously." Dylan kissed him gently, lips so warm and good on his.

They hadn't known each other for more than a day. They couldn't be talking about ridiculousness like this, but.... Dylan. His Dylan.

Rey grinned, his entire body buzzing with happiness. "So do we take this to the others?"

"Send the link to James. We'll all meet once everyone has done their bit. Mick will call."

"Okay. I can do that."

Dylan dragged one hand down along his spine, the touch almost stinging.

He moaned, his joy turning easily to need in the wake of the touch. "Dylan."

"I know. I know." Dylan kissed him again, letting him feel a little ache.

"I'm going to get you in trouble, distracting you." He felt dizzy, felt like the world was spinning.

"Maybe. I think the guys will cut us some slack." Dylan squeezed one of his asscheeks, sliding that hand under him easily. "They'll have to understand. I need to touch you again. I need to make sure our bond grows."

Dylan groaned and nuzzled into his neck, teeth threatening.

Rey moaned, his body warming, his cock hardening in a rush. How could this be happening? Bond? Yes, that was exactly what they had. Just like the mate bond he'd read about. Apparently, in the early stages, a bonded pair had sex.

Often.

"Tell me you need me." Dylan's voice was pure, deep growl.

"I do." He climbed into Dylan's lap, which seemed to be his new habit.

"Good." Dylan kissed him, arching him over one arm, stretching him out.

He felt exposed but also too clothed. Damn it, why was he dressed?

He swore he could feel Dylan's rough laughter bouncing inside his head. Dylan kissed his chin, his neck, then licked at his skin.

The bite, when it came, was blindingly fast and deep enough to ache. Dylan liked the biting part, so he grunted, wiggling until he could sink his teeth into Dylan's shoulder.

Dylan growled, stood, and carried him to the back. To that little bed.

Laughing, he wrapped around Dylan, wondering if Dylan even had a place of his own.

"Don't worry. Just let me touch you," Dylan said, panting for him.

"I'm not worried, love." In fact, he worried least of all in Dylan's arms.

"Mmm... love. Yes."

He blinked, but he'd meant it. Dylan was a key that unlocked him.

Dylan laid him down, then came down on top of him, rubbing against him.

"Dylan, we still have clothes on."

"All in good time, sweetheart."

He chuckled, tracing Dylan's ear with his tongue. "So mean to me."

"I am. Vicious wolf." Dylan pressed one thigh down between his legs.

"My vicious wo—" Oh. Oh, that was so hot. He bucked, his body zinging as if he'd touched a live wire.

"Your vicious wolf. Look at you, baby. You make me hard."

"Thank God. You have an amazing dick." Was that... slutty?

Dylan hooted. "Thank you. Want to see it?"

"I want to see it. Suck it. Ride it. Touch it. All the its."

"Please." Dylan rose up off him, tearing at his clothes.

Apparently this was the "in good time" part.

"Don't make me beat you, foxy." Dylan seemed like he was in such a good mood.

He stuck his tongue out at Dylan, wiggling it madly. Making promises with it.

Dylan bit the tip, which was a fine maneuver in its own right. That took skill.

He gasped, staring into those warm, near-golden eyes. He could see the wolf in them, feel the contained power, and he reveled in it.

Dylan bent again, this time biting him so deliberately he almost came. He was going to have a bruise on his neck.

He heard it so clearly. So loud in his head. *Mine.*

"Yours." He could no more deny that than he could stop breathing.

Whatever this was, it was theirs.

"Mates, sweetheart. We're mates."

"Touch me." He arched into Dylan's body, begging him for more.

"Anything." Dylan stripped him down as well before running both big hands down his body. He felt dizzy, totally at the will of his instincts. He hoped they weren't pouring out pheromones.

They probably were. Had Dylan locked the door?

"Pay attention," Dylan said, growling.

"Make me."

His eyes went wide. Had he said that?

"Oh, I will." Dylan pressed him down, grabbing both his

wrists in one hand to hold Rey's hands over his head. "Gonna make you crazy."

"Dylan...." Rey stretched up tall and as long as he could, lifting his chin, begging for another bite.

The low growl he got raised the hair on the back of his neck. Oh, that was amazing. That sound. Need and Alphaness and heat. That big body covered his, and he panted, the slide of their skin making him overheat.

"Mine, Rey. My mate." Dylan's free hand dragged over his skin, cupping his balls, circling his cock.

"Yes." He arched into the touches, and Dylan gripped the base of his dick hard enough to make him grunt, then tugged all the way to the tip.

"Dylan!" His cry was sharp, and he spread wide, his thighs shaking.

"You smell like home. Like all the good things. Sharp and salty." Dylan stroked until he had to grit his teeth and curl his toes to keep from coming. "Good. Good, wait for me. You...." Dylan bent his head and bit again.

"Oh." He scratched at Dylan's back. "Hurry up, then."

"I'm almost there." Dylan drove against him, hand trapped between them.

He surged up, bit Dylan's earlobe, and tugged.

"Uh! Now." Dylan squeezed his cock, and that sent him right over the edge. He shot against his mate, his balls emptying in a rush.

Dylan's deep, musky scent flooded him, that come sliding over his cock and belly. So hot. They were perfect together. Mates, he supposed. He had no idea that could even happen.

He didn't really care. He was just glad it had happened.

Dylan nuzzled just under Rey's ear. "Yes."

"I can smell you, us." Rey groaned softly. "Crazy."

"Mates by scent, hmm?"

"I have no idea how to be a wolf."

Dylan snorted. "My pack has two cats and a bear."

"And a fox," he pointed out.

"Right. The only traditional thing is that Mick is a big bad wolf who huffs and puffs. He loves us all."

Somewhere across the room, Dylan's phone started playing "Red Riding Hood."

"Uh-oh." Rey figured that was someone pointing out that it was time to stop canoodling.

Did people still canoodle?

"Shit." Dylan rolled off him, wiping off on the sheets. He lumbered over to grab up his phone. "Yeah, boss?"

That muscled ass made him stare and possibly....

Oh, that was worth a.... He grabbed his phone and took a picture. Yummy.

Dylan glared at him over one shoulder. "Uh-huh. I know. Yes, we were. Well, tough. Okay, be down in a mo."

Rey zoomed in, took another shot because that big, rangy body was so perfectly lovely.

"Mick, I need to go. No. No, I'm going to beat him."

"Only if you can catch me." Ooh. Balls!

"Rey!" Dylan barked out his name, coming at him like a steam train just getting moving.

He leapt over the desk, spinning in the desk chair, snapping photos all the way. "I'm so instagramming you."

"You are not!" Dylan roared like a fairy-tale dragon, hands up to reach for him.

Okay, that was hot as anything, and he couldn't remember ever having so much fun in his life. He ran in circles, always just one step ahead of his lover, until Dylan turned back on him, grabbing him up to swing him around. He laughed into their kiss, rejoicing in Dylan's strength.

"Mmm."

A knock sounded at the outer door. "Dylan? Did the crocs

find you? It sounds like a scene of unimaginable violence in there."

Dylan shouted with laughter. "No, Kit! We'll be right there!"

"Good. You can't keep him all to yourself, you know. We all need to get to know him."

Oh, he wasn't sure anyone was going to get to know him like Dylan did. In fact, he would be rather put out if they did.

"I know, buddy. Be right down." Dylan winked at him. "Grab the laptop. Uh, after clothes."

"Clothes would be lovely." He took a selfie with them both.

"Freak." Dylan goosed him. "I love it. Love you."

His eyes widened, the words ringing in his ears. "It's real, right? Even though we don't know each other hardly? It's okay?"

"It's real. I have faith." Dylan stopped everything, staring into his eyes. There lay a wealth of certainty there, a deep meaning.

"I can't wait to learn things about you."

"What's your favorite food? Besides raisins?" Dylan pulled on the rumpled clothes right off the floor.

"Potato chips. Nuts. Crunchy things. You?" He got his jeans on.

"Mmm. Peanut butter. Hamburgers. Weird Colorado meats, like elk."

"Elk burgers," he moaned. Gracious, he did love game meat.

"We'll go. I know a great place. No crocs allowed."

Rey licked his lips, his belly all but gnawing at his spine. "How can I be hungry after all that food we ate?"

"Good sex. Great sex," Dylan corrected himself.

"Right." Rey could get used to that so quickly. Not just the sex and hunger but the rollicking adventure of Apex Investigations. Rey got dressed before grabbing the laptop. "Is it weird to go barefoot?"

"Nah. We'll go to Mick's apartment, I bet."

"Where do you live? You've seen my old place, such as it is, with the fish stink and green water." Rey grimaced.

"I live about five blocks from here. I walk to work." Dylan grinned. "It's great. An industrial place they made into apartments."

"Oh? That sounds amazing. Will you take me to see?"

"I will." Dylan led him out, then through a warren of hallways.

"Does Mick own the whole building?"

"He does. He rents to Kit and Brock too. James is in a weird place over in the low-rent district on Colfax. Very hoarder house."

"Techie types can be that way. I just love dens. I like things to be organized."

"I do too. I mean, I let my clothes pile up. They don't stink." Dylan knocked on a heavy door.

"My place didn't stink until the crocs moved in," he agreed. Musk was one thing. They were predators. Nastiness was another thing altogether.

"Come in, you two. Tell me you washed." Mick was very frowny and growly.

"Oh. No. We did wipe off," Dylan said breezily.

"I only have so many clothes," Rey pointed out.

"Brock brought you more." Mick gave them the greasy eyeball.

"Stop it, Mick. We'll go have a shower after." Dylan bared his teeth.

"I want you and James here with the rest of us permanently." Mick bumped against Dylan's shoulder, a move so wolfy it was akin to watching a documentary.

"I have a place, boss."

Rey shot Dylan a look. Oh, this was like a constant argument, something that they'd all been over. He wondered if Mick would want him there too if he stayed like Dylan had asked him to.

"I have a place for both of you, and the rent is better than your place." Mick crossed his arms over his chest, puffing up.

"Can we growl about this later?" James asked. "Hey, Rey, good work."

"Thank you." Rey smiled at James, relieved at the change of subject. "Did you find out who owned the property?"

"You were right. Patel Inc., and not even hiding behind a holding company."

"Traced back directly?" Mick nodded. "Excellent. We can arrange a meet."

"For what? Just to give him his SIM card back?" Rey wasn't certain he followed the logic.

"No, to get the authorities in on it. We have the video, but a confession would be nice." Mick wandered around.

"Oh. Cool." Rey didn't know how any of this worked. He mined information, not trouble, so he wasn't at all certain about meet-ups and police and tigers.

"This is where we shine," Dylan said. "We'll make sure no one goes in alone."

"Okay. Well, if you have my back."

"We do."

Nods came from all around the room. Everyone seemed to be behind him, and he thought maybe it wasn't just a job. Rey was part of the pack now.

It didn't mean he wasn't frightened, but he'd figure it out; he had to. He could face Patel. He would have to, because the man was trying to kill him with crocodiles.

Hopefully a fox was too small for a tiger to take notice of. Perhaps together they were big enough to take on a big cat like Patel.

Still, that was better than having to do it all alone.

———

Dylan knocked on Mick's office door about an hour after the last team meeting. The man had made the call to Patel, and Dylan wanted to see what the verdict was. He and Rey had showered, and now Rey was with James, making maps and getting satellite images and shit.

He wanted to know what the plan was. Hell, he needed to know so he could gird his loins.

"Hey, Dylan, come on in. He's willing to meet. I told him we have the chip." Mick looked less than thrilled but grimly satisfied.

"Okay. I hear you. When and where?" And he wanted was Rey left here with James, despite the fact that Rey thought he was coming along.

"Sixteenth Street mall. I figured that was so damn public he wouldn't chance the crocs." Mick's expression was moving into pretty tickled now. He did love an adventure.

"Oh, that's a great place to make the trade. Open. No water. Nowhere to hide."

"Exactly. Close to the capitol so security is good...." Mick preened a little.

"Right. When?"

"Tomorrow at noon. I refused to do it in the dark. Pissed the son of a bitch right off."

Dylan chuckled. "Good for you. Okay, so what can I do to help prepare?" He sat in the chair across from Mick's desk. "I feel trapped in here."

"I want to make sure we have a tactical plan, everyone is armed. I want eyes on the whole place." Mick ticked off each point on his fingers.

"You got it. I'll get with Brock and Kit." He was about to

stand when Mick held up a hand. Dylan sank back into his chair. "What?"

"What's it going to take for you to move in?" Mick asked. The very evenness of his tone meant he was through joking and threatening.

"Don't you think having us all in one place is the easiest way to attack us all at once?" They'd had this discussion a dozen times a month for years.

"I worry. You're pack, and now you have a mate to protect."

"About that...." He took a deep breath, clearing his mind. "We're good?"

"We are? Who's we?" Mick frowned.

"You and me, man. Even with Rey."

"Oh!" Mick's expression cleared up. "Yes. Why would I object to Rey?" Mick grimaced. "I mean, I did think he was a faker to begin with, but I know better now."

"He's amazing, isn't he?" Dylan grinned at his Alpha, so pleased he could bust.

"I like him. He's quiet but devious. And clean. You know he did the dishes with Kit from the hamburger feast?" Mick asked.

"Did he? He likes Kit."

"I do too." Mick winked. "I got to admit, Dylan, I'm worried. Those crocs are something."

"They're awful. I have to tell you, Rey seemed to know they were out there when we parked."

Mick's eyes narrowed, one eyebrow lifting. "What? He knew?"

"No, no. Sensed. I mean, he sensed it."

That made Mick scowl harder. "Weird. I mean, some guys do have a sixth sense. I think Brock has warrior timing and James has electro-philia."

"Right?" They all had something clever about them, or they sure seemed to. That was why they were a team.

That was why they were a family. "Well, we'll stay here until this is over, anyway. But I don't know about moving in. I don't like being a singular target, boss."

"I know." Mick sighed. "I wish there was a better solution, but we're urban or we can't do our job."

"Well, for now, we're here. We'll revisit once we deal with this croc situation."

"Yeah. Man, who knew?"

They shared a grin, because crocs. In Denver. It boggled the mind, really.

"All right. I'll get with Brock. Holler if you need me."

Mick waved him off, so he went looking for grumpy kitty.

He played the find-the-kitty game with himself. He had a knack for finding people. He didn't think about it too hard, and he wasn't silly enough to think that he was psychic. He just paid attention, noticing details when he needed to. Writing them down.

"You start with the obvious," he muttered, peeking into Brock's office. No dice. So, not obvious. "Gym." Hands in his pockets, he whistled his way to the gym on the lower floor. Brock worked out often when he was on a puzzle.

The sound of Brock's fists hitting the heavy bag came to him, the noise rhythmic and steady. Familiar. Dylan wandered into the room, wishing he'd picked up a doughnut or something. Watching Brock work out made him hungry.

Brock worked the bag with a steadily increasing pace, the pounding growing faster, harder.

Dylan plopped down on a weight bench, waiting. Admiring. A dead straight man would admire Brock like this—hot, shining with sweat, focused. Yum.

"Stop drooling at me, Dylan."

"Hey, you wouldn't work this hard if you didn't want people to look," Dylan teased.

"I work this hard because I have to protect you and all my clients."

"I don't live here, Brock." Everyone seemed to think he couldn't take care of himself.

"Mick wants you here because he's the pack Alpha, Dylan. Not because he thinks you're incompetent."

"And you want to protect me because?"

"You're my *amigo*." That frown was epic.

Dylan nodded. "I am, at that. Why are you so pissy about me and Rey hooking up?" He wanted to know, to clear the air.

"I don't like foxes. I had a bad experience."

"What happened?" He knew Brock had been in a brutal relationship, but all the details had never been explained.

Brock shook his head. "Doesn't matter. It's over."

"It matters to me, honey. Not just because Rey is my guy now, but because I can tell it makes you so unhappy." He was turning all touchy-feely. Being mated was putting him in touch with his Sears softer side.

"I like your Rey. He's a good one, no?" That was a huge thing for Brock to say.

"Thanks, man. He's.... I've never met anyone like him."

"That's how it's supposed to be, when you're mated."

"How does everyone know?" He wasn't upset, just curious. Was there some kind of a sign?

"Fuck if I know. My breed doesn't mate."

"Bullshit." The word popped out. Foxes didn't mate with wolves and dire crocs didn't exist.

Brock spun around, eyes flashing with a deep, deep pain. "What did you say?"

"I said bullshit." He stood, going to bump chests with Mr. Kitty. "There's someone out there."

"You're just stupid in lust right now. You've got mating on

the brain." Brock pushed back, damn near knocking him down despite being a third smaller than him.

"No, I just never believed in the mate bond. If a fox and wolf can do it, so can you."

"I'm not interested. You can learn all about it for me. I lost two men I thought were mates. That's enough." Brock spun him around, walking him toward the wall.

"Hey. We're supposed to be working together on the meet." Dylan would let it go. For now.

"Yeah, we just need to struggle it out a little, Dylan." Brock gave him a pleading look over one shoulder.

"Oh! Well, why didn't you say so." He launched himself at Brock's unprotected back. Brock rolled him over one shoulder, leaving him crashing to the mat.

His breath whooshed out, but he could hardly just lie there. No, he spun his legs, kicking into enough leverage to get up.

"Very nice." Brock leapt, tackling him.

He grunted, letting gravity drag them both down. Dylan could never match Brock's speed, but he had weight to use on his side.

They wrestled, both of them well-matched, neither of them wanting to hurt each other. Dylan went flying more than once, but Brock ended up on the mat a few times too.

Finally James's voice sounded over the intercom. "Enough playing, you two. Time to work."

"You got something for us? How can we help set up eyes and all?" They were both panting but ready to work, all their angst worked out.

"We're going to hack into the security system at the mall. It's an older system, totally easy to piggyback onto."

"Parking?" Brock tossed him a towel.

"Thanks."

"I have a set of maps up here, and they're on your phones."

"What about the crocs? Rey said eyes and throats. What other weak spots?"

"Eyes and throats are the big ones. At least, we think so. There's no database on these guys," James muttered.

"Where's Rey?" Dylan asked, because he hadn't heard his lover over the speaker.

"I think he went to his car? He wanted to clean it up."

"James! You let him?" Dylan raced out of the gym, heading for the parking lot. Rey should never be outside alone right now.

"He's an adult, Dylan." James sounded uncertain now, though.

Right. A lithe, slender adult who was not well-trained and was his, dammit. "You should have called me," he shouted, banging out the side door to the parking lot.

Rey spun around and stood, fetching up against the open door, his mate swaying and grabbing his head.

"Sweetheart? What are you doing?" He moved fast, hands loose but ready.

"I was cleaning up. You startled me. I hit my head."

"Oh shit. Let me help." Dylan slowed, trotting to Rey. "Can I see?"

"Uh-huh." Rey reached for him, swaying just a little bit.

"Oh, you hit hard. Come on, let's go inside and get some ice and some aspirin."

"Okay. I was trying to make myself useful." Rey sounded a little put out.

He tucked Rey under his arm.

"Useful is cool. But no one should be out here alone. We have clothes and stuff inside that Brock brought in." He wasn't growly, just worried. In-in-in.

"In-in-in." Rey nodded.

"That's it." He breathed a sigh of relief once they made it inside. He wasn't one to be afraid of the big bad anything, but they needed to plan for stuff. To calculate risks.

"I smell blood." That was Kit appearing out of nowhere, that nose in the know as always. "Who's hurt?"

"Rey hit his head. Check him out for me?" Kit had a real knack for medic stuff.

"I'm fine," Rey protested.

"You're bleeding."

"Dylan...." Rey looked to him.

"Nope. Policy. If you're bleeding, Kit checks you out." Those were the rules, and Dylan intended to bring Rey into the fold.

Rey pouted, which was the cutest thing ever.

He swooped down and took a kiss, then popped Rey into Kit's hands.

"Oh, Rey. You did whack yourself." Kit shook his head. "It's gonna bruise like a bitch."

"I'm not broken, though," Rey said plaintively. "My car...."

"Not that I can tell, but I recommend some ibuprofen and rest. You're gonna be dizzy." Kit grabbed an alcohol swab from the backpack he carried everywhere and cleaned Rey quickly, ignoring his fox's hiss of discomfort.

Dylan could almost feel the cold sting himself.

As soon as Kit was done, Dylan grabbed his fox and headed toward his office. He needed to hold Rey, just rest with his hand on Rey's thigh.

"You keep carrying me," Rey pointed out.

"I do. Is it weird?" Dylan opened his office door.

"I don't know. Is it strange that it's a little hot?"

"Nope." A huge grin split his face. "Totally natural."

Rey leaned into him, breath warm on his neck. It sent tingles all through him. He wanted Rey all over again. He thought maybe they were cementing their bond. Mick seemed to think so.

He sat and Rey stayed with him, right there, close and warm.

Rey leaned against him, tracing patterns on his chest with one hand.

Soft sounds filled the air, foreign and familiar, all at once. His vocal fox.

Humming in return, Dylan stroked Rey's back, up and down, the motion meant to comfort. Rey melted, a sweet chirruping purr sounding.

"Mmm... listen to you. Sweet lover."

"You make my head feel better."

Dylan smiled. "Do you heal better as a fox? We could shift." He loved all that red fur.

"Oh, it hurts you. I heard you when you shifted back that time." Rey began to stroke him, petting him. Then the grooming and nuzzling began.

"Not as much when you're around. Maybe your ability to shift easily is rubbing off through the bond."

Rey was stripping him down, baring him. He had a feeling Rey liked foxiness. Hadn't he said he stayed that way a lot at home?

"Do I need to get you chew things?"

"I can chew on you, but I love the rope bones."

"Well, nibble on me this time, and we'll outfit you."

Rey chuckled softly, lips brushing his jaw.

"Okay, you too. Nakey time so we can get furry and snuggle." Maybe groom. He loved to groom, but shifting had been so bad before Rey that he'd been reluctant to join the guys in the cuddle piles.

"Mm-hmm. Naked." Rey wasn't stripping down, he noticed.

"Not just me." He tugged at Rey's shirt, wanting skin. He

wasn't needing, at least not in that hard-core way, but no sense ruining their clothes.

"Of course." Rey stood up and struggled out of his shoes, his jeans.

"You got it?" Dylan steadied his mate, not wanting Rey dizzy or queasy. Poor head.

"Yeah. It'll be okay. It's just a goose egg."

"That still sucks, sweetie." Listen to him. He rubbed noses with his lover. "Ready?" He closed his eyes, hoping it still sucked less than usual. Maybe it had been that it was an emergency and this would be super painful....

"Ready." Rey touched him, hands on his chest, and his wolf came in a wild, dizzying rush.

He sat on the floor, his tail thumping, and waited for Rey. His tongue lolled, and he was so damn tickled. It took Rey no time at all to shift, to curl into his fur and nuzzle close.

Panting, he rubbed his face along Rey's fur, breathing deep of Rey's scent, which was imprinted on his brain now. He would know it anywhere, find it anywhere.

Rey vocalized for him, singing happily. Rey was cheerful, fearless, moving in to groom him without a hint of worry. There wasn't a bit of shame or fear, even though Dylan was easily twice his size, that Dylan would hurt him.

Thank God.

Dylan nosed him over, muzzle buried in Rey's belly.

Rey kicked all four paws, making this little bark that sounded just like laughter. Oh, beautiful pup!

He licked and chewed, smoothing the heavy white fur so carefully.

Not much longer and Rey was gnawing on him, little nibbles and scrapes. The tiny paws worked out snarls, Rey licking and smoothing his fur, and all the while, that song filled his mind.

Mostly it was DylanmateDylanmate, even if there were no

real words to it. The mantra filled him with pride and love. There was a simple happiness to it, a sweet surety.

Dylan closed his eyes, letting Rey chew on his ear. Those sharp teeth never closed down too hard.

His paws were carefully explored, his muzzle and whiskers adored. He had never been so wanted, so cared for.

Dylan rolled to his back this time, letting Rey crawl on top of him. There was nothing wrong with baring his throat and belly to his mate.

Once he was totally groomed, Rey slipped back on the ground with a happy, satisfied sound.

He nosed Rey up on the bed, because why not? It had gotten more use in the last week than it had in years.

Then he let himself lick and lap, exploring Rey, sharing their scent. Sweet mate. Dylan was still stunned by how fast, and how necessary, all this was.

Rey was in his bones, in his marrow.

They were connected. He rumbled, stretching his feet. Oh, that felt good. Rey snuggled in with a soft sigh, curling into his belly.

They would rest. Heal. Well, Rey would. Dylan was feeling kinda fabulous. Even with all the weirdness hanging over their heads.

He'd found a mate, just walked in and found him. Well, his mate had walked into Mick's office to cause trouble.

He snorted, his tail moving a little. Wagging.

Rey lifted his head, nosing his muzzle. He licked Rey, and they both settled down, ready to doze, he thought.

Rey's chin settled on his paws, the bright eyes closing.

Yes, rest. Then they had a tiger to catch by the tail.

EIGHT

A hard knock sounded and Rey leapt up with a sharp bark, warning Dylan that someone was here.

Someone wanted into their den!

Dylan rose, stretching, sniffing the air. That tail lifted and wagged, and Dylan barked.

The door opened, so they'd forgotten to lock it. "Pizza downstairs. Get it while it's hot." Kit smiled back and forth between them, dark brown eyes twinkling.

Oh! Kit! Rey ran over to the big bear and jumped into the sweet man's arms.

"Hey, Rey. Look how cute you are. I could eat you up. Figuratively, I mean. I'm a black bear. I don't eat a lot of meat as a bear. As a human I'm all over the all-meat pizza down there." Kit hugged him carefully, scratching his ears. "And look at you, Dylan! All wolfed out!"

Dylan barked again, just grinning a lupine grin.

"I'm so pleased. Come now. Pizza."

A low whine came from Dylan, who sounded hungry.

Oh.

How wonderful to hear Dylan's wolf sounds and know what they meant.

"I'll see you downstairs." Kit let him down, then closed the door.

All he had to do was think of his man, and his body changed, his fur falling away. He stood, shaking his arms. "Come on, love. Pizza."

He hoped Dylan could shift easily. He moved over to the bed, reaching out, fingers dragging over Dylan's fur.

Dylan licked his wrist, the touch warm and rough.

"Tickles. How can I help you?" Rey smiled, his joy bubbling out of him.

Dylan's pretty eyes closed, and Rey felt the air expand and contract. Dylan was trying.

"Mmm... gorgeous man."

Dylan went all man, naked on the floor for a moment on all fours.

"Uhn." The sound escaped him, raw and honest.

Dylan laughed. "Thank you. I'd bow, but that's weird sitting on the floor."

"Right? And skin sticks where fur doesn't."

"Exactly." Dylan climbed to his feet. "We don't want to miss the pizza. The place we order from is amazing." Dylan rummaged for clothes, then handed Rey some clean stuff from his pile.

"Sounds good. I'm going to give Patel the SIM card tomorrow, correct?"

"Not you, you're staying here with James." Dylan found a shirt.

"What?"

"Mick and I are going to make the exchange. You're the civilian, sweetheart." Dylan disappeared into a polo shirt for a moment, his voice muffled.

"I thought I would.... What are you exchanging? How do we know they'll stop?"

"We don't." Dylan shrugged, then pulled on his pants. "And we're not giving him anything. The cops will be there. We have that video. They just need him to admit he needs it. Then they can move in."

"Oh? Of course. That makes perfect sense." Okay, so he was a little bit of an idiot, wasn't he, thinking Dylan needed his help.

"We work with the police a good deal." Dylan smiled and came to kiss him. "Clothes, Rey. That way we can sort of all explain to you what will happen."

"You have to be dressed for that?" he teased.

"Unless you want the guys to tease you about how pale you are. I would show you off, no doubt." Dylan winked at him, which made him blush.

"Compared to you guys, I'm a ninety-pound weakling."

"You're gorgeous. So pretty." Dylan petted Rey's belly.

Rey hid his blush in his shirt. That was good to hear.

"Okay." Dylan wrapped an arm around him as soon as he was dressed. "Pizza!" They trundled out into the hall.

"Pizza ho!" Rey snorted and followed his nose. He could get over feeling a little duped about the exchange. He'd misunderstood.

It led him back to Mick's place. He wanted to see Kit's apartment too, but that seemed intrusive, just to ask.

"So three of you live here and two don't?"

"Yeah. James is a little... private. I just had my place before I came to work here, and I don't like the idea of us all being an easy target." Dylan chuckled. "Not that Mick doesn't reel us all in during a crisis."

"Oh, so I'm not the only crisis?" That was comforting in its own way.

"God, no. We had this one client who'd been hired by someone in South America to kill Brock...."

"Ack!" For whatever reason, Rey thought Brock was a little amazing. Genuinely.

Not Dylan amazing, of course, but pretty wondrous.

"He's pissed off a lot of people over the years." Dylan knocked at Mick's door.

"Oh. I guess that happens. It happened to me and I didn't even mean for it to."

"Brock meant to do it."

"What did I do now, *família*?" Brock asked from right behind them.

"Pissed people off." Dylan didn't seem all that unhappy to say it.

"Fuck off, puppy-man."

"Not us. When those jungle guys came after you, dick." Dylan poked Brock's chest.

"Oh. Yeah. That was a shit situation. Fun, though. Lots of weird assholes with big teeth."

Rey thought he knew about weird assholes with big teeth, especially recently.

"Sounds like now." Dylan echoed his thoughts. "Pizza."

Kit opened the door to let them in. "Pizza. That is that magic word."

"Isn't it? It's like a... universal healer." Rey loved coming out of his shell and teasing. No group of people had ever... gotten him.

Kit gave Rey an approving smile. "Yes! I like that it's so customizable."

"I love it all. Omnivore, you know." Rey gave Kit a thumbs-up.

Kit nodded happily. "I know! Green peppers, mushrooms, onions!"

"Olives," he moaned.

"All the good stuff." Dylan hustled them inside. "We're leaving Mick alone with it."

"Mick and James. James can eat pizzas whole in seconds." Brock's smile was toothy as hell.

"Oh no! Let's save it." Rey laughed out loud, because Kit linked arms with him, zooming him to the little kitchen.

There were a dozen pizzas, Cokes, garlic bread, wings and sauce. God. Starving. He was starving all of a sudden.

"It's all the running amok," Kit said when his belly growled.

"Amok amok amok!" *Please get the Looney Toons joke. Please.*

When the entire group started amoking along, Rey couldn't stop grinning. They were his tribe, for real, and he was so... happy.

Dylan squeezed his butt, then slid past him to get drinks.

They put the pizzas between them, and then, before they ate, they all stood together, raised their glasses.

"To Rey," Dylan said.

"To us." That was Mick. "All of us."

"Ditto," James said.

"Grrr, argh." That was Brock.

"Fantastic." Kit grinned at him, and he began to laugh.

"Allons-y!" Rey exclaimed in the words of the tenth doctor.

"Oh God, Doctor Who." Dylan and Mick exchanged pained looks.

"They can have marathons," Brock murmured.

"That'll keep them busy while we play poker." Mick shook his head, his smile fond.

"True." Dylan winked at Rey when he made an outraged noise.

"I would love to. We'll make vats of popcorn." Kit was just beaming.

"Oh, yum. I'm coming to sit with you." Rey grabbed another piece of pizza with both kinds of olives on it, then a wing.

They all fell on the food, munching and laughing and teasing each other.

Rey hadn't known he was so lonely, because he'd felt fairly fulfilled in his job.

Now he knew, and he would worry he would lose this soon, but Dylan had said full-time. Him. Dylan. Them.

They could be an us.

Dylan glanced over at him, smiled at him, and he felt the look everywhere. It had heat rising in his cheeks and a deep happiness coming up in his belly. Oh, he was so lost.

"You two are so cute," Kit whispered.

Brock made gagging noises until James stuffed a wing into his mouth.

"I'm jealous. Seriously." Kit grinned at Rey, the expression warm.

"Thank you, Kit." He got it; he'd be jealous too if he wasn't the one newly mated.

"No problem. Oh, ranch dip." Kit grabbed some breadsticks and a cup of ranch. They could all put the food away.

Rey handed Dylan a piece of sausage and pepperoni, his mate humming his thanks.

Brock pushed some extra olives on his plate. Oh. How sweet. Grumpy kitty was dear.

"Thank you." Oh, he'd missed this—being a part of a den, which he hadn't had since childhood.

"*Não tem problema.*" Brock's ears were all red.

Mick chuckled, drawing his gaze. He got a wink, so he figured even Mick wasn't going to kick him out. This was the best. Well, the pizza was pretty good too.

They ate all the pizza, all the breadsticks, all the wings.

In fact, they ate the cinnamon knots Mick pulled out from

the kitchen and laid on the table just when they thought they were all done.

Rey groaned when they polished those off. "Oh God. I need to work out."

"Brock will happily add you to the list of people he tosses around," Mick said.

"No tossing my mate." Oh, Dylan's growl was hot as hell.

"No?" Brock waggled his black eyebrows. "Could be fun."

"Nope. Wrestle with James. Both kitties." Rey nodded sagely, as if that solved all the world's problems.

Brock snorted. "If I need a challenge, I'll go for Mick."

"I'll exercise with you, Rey," Kit offered. "Long walks and naps are amazing."

"They so are." Rey beamed, and Dylan grumbled, which made him laugh. He had to hide it in his Coke. Dylan wasn't mad. He could hear the proud, happy song in his head coming from his mate.

He wasn't the long nap type anyway, at least when he wasn't on the run. He was more the clean the whole world and reorganize the pantry type. That could totally be exercise.... Maybe he should ask Dylan what apartment Mick wanted to give them. Him. Dylan. Whatever. He could clean it up and make it nice so they had a place to stay when they were on lockdown. That cot was small.

Cramped.

Would that be weird? Would that be like telling Mick he wanted to move in and, perhaps, undermining Dylan? Maybe he should just organize his car. That would be better. Organize his car and clean up the back seat.

Dylan put a hand on his arm, tugging him back around to sit next to his mate instead of by Kit. "You want to move in with me? For real?"

"Not because I lost my place. Because it's you. You said you wanted me to stay...."

"Of course. We can ask." Dylan squeezed his hand.

"Did we miss something?" Mick was staring at them, a shrewd look in his eyes.

"No. No, we're just talking, making plans, right, Dylan?"

"Right."

"Creeeepy," James singsonged. "Sometimes you're not talking out loud."

The little sound rang through his brain.

He grinned. "Sorry, James. We'll try to keep it to a dull roar." Not that he could help it. It was all too new and he was so in love with Dylan....

And he knew that he should doubt, but he also knew that he always trusted his gut. Always.

That had kept him alive recently and kept him in work before that.

"Are we gonna talk business or nap?" James asked.

"I vote nap." Kit yawned hugely.

"Dylan and I just napped. I think." Time was running together, the outside world not at all a factor in here.

"We can all shift, then nap. Together." Kit's suggestion was gentle but needy. "Tomorrow is going to be hard."

"That sounds great, kiddo." Mick gave first Dylan, then him, a stern look.

Oh! That made sense. What if they all had to shift together when things weren't so calm? They should know the scent of his fox, the feel of his fur.

"I'm happy with that," Rey murmured.

Dylan took his hand. "Rey is an easy shifter. So smooth."

"Lucky." Kit shook his head. "I'm slow. The cats are so fast."

"It was hurting Dylan," Rey said cautiously. "I think it's easier now?"

"It is. It still takes some thought."

Mick nodded, offering Dylan a wolfy grin. "I like this—us all grooming. Together."

"Weirdo." Brock stood. "I'll go change in the bathroom."

"You're so modest." James winked broadly.

"I don't want any of you getting jealous of how well-endowed I am." Brock's lip curled, and he walked off, head held high.

"Scars," Mick said softly.

"Oh, is that why?" Kit looked stricken. "Poor Brock."

Oh, dear man. Rey would love on him. And Kit. And James and Mick, if the wolf would allow it.

Dylan's low growl gave him the shivers. Then Dylan's smile lit up the room, and Dylan stood, tugging off his shirt. "Come on, you louts. I'm stuffed with food and ready to be lazy."

Rey took Dylan's shirt, folded it, then pulled off his own.

They all stripped down, but no one really looked, which was lovely and gave Rey confidence. The air began to shimmer, the magic of shifting happening all around him. He changed immediately, his fox totally responsive and eager. As soon as he shifted, he ran to Dylan, calling his wolf.

Dylan met him, muzzle against his, whiskers so much rougher than his.

He sang softly, then Dylan nudged him over to Mick. Mick was a huge timber wolf, lovely, and Rey bowed. His breed didn't have the same hierarchy, but he understood how it worked.

Mick nuzzled his cheeks, sharing scent. Accepting him.

He sang happily, letting the whole pack know he was there and pleased. A huge black panther came to him and grabbed him by the nape, taking him from Mick and beginning to groom him with a rough, huge tongue.

He chittered, stretching his paws and swiveling his ears.

Brock nibbled and bit, making him tingle all over. Dylan nosed Brock, maybe too hard, but no one growled or snapped.

As soon as Brock backed off, he was scooped up in one vast paw. Bear. Oh. Big bear. He sort of... dangled.

Kit seemed huge, even though he claimed to be a little black bear. That paw was bigger than Rey's head. Kit held him close, grunting and huffing against him. He had to wiggle, testing that grip, but soon he got fascinated by Kit's scent, his nose stuck deep in Kit's fur.

James crawled into Kit's arms with him, taking his time to groom them both. Brock was working on Dylan and Mick was looking on, pride emanating from him.

Someone loved this pack very much. Very much.

Finally, though, his mate came up to Kit and barked, demanding his release, his presence. Him.

Kit let him go so he could go to Dylan, who gently bit his neck, then flopped down on top of him with a thud.

He snorted, his whiskers flapping. Yes. He was Dylan's mate.

Dylan carefully groomed him, chuffing softly in his ear. So careful, so gentle. Dylan was a treasure. He believed. He didn't understand, but he believed.

Rey blew out a happy sigh and relaxed, settling deep into the carpet.

One by one, the others joined them, Kit and Mick last, forming a protective circle around them all.

He pushed into Dylan's soft belly fur and slept.

Nine

"Okay, here's how it lays out." Mick had in hand a schematic that James had printed out for them. Mick liked hard copy rather than the screen Brock preferred. "The meet is here." Mick pointed with a pen. "He thinks I want money. That I'm not just protecting Rey, but that I'm getting greedy."

"Where do you want me, boss? I smell enough like Rey that I should be confusing." Dylan was ready to get this whole thing done.

"I want you downwind. He's in that fancy-ass mansion they just redid up by the botanic garden, so he should come in here. I want you here." Mick circled a spot, and Dylan inclined his head.

"Solid. And Rey and James stay here to monitor comms."

Both Brock and Mick nodded, but it was Mick who spoke. "Absolutely. We don't need him in any danger, and James is still sore from the bullshit with those badgers."

"Yeah, no. Badgers. *Cristo.*" Brock shook his head. "That was strangely almost fatal."

"Those bastards are tough." Mick clicked his tongue.

But they weren't croc tough.

"Yeah. Why do we do this again?" Dylan asked. As a cop, he'd rarely dealt with other shifters. The occasional wolf gone rogue. Humans could be monstrous enough.

"Money. Cold hard cash." Mick chuffed at him, blowing his lips.

"Right. I make a mint." Though Mick was fair, and the money was way better than a cop's salary.

"I do." Brock waggled his eyebrows. "But I'm good."

He and Mick laughed together, leaning back in their chairs. "We all good?" Mick asked. "Know what our roles are?"

"Yep." Brock rubbed his thumb over his chin, fingering a scar there. "You play bad *homem* and we back you up."

Rey came into the war room, shaking his head. "I think this is a bad idea. I think you should cancel."

"What?" Dylan rose, his instinct to comfort Rey popping to the fore. He could feel waves of worry pouring off his mate.

"I just... please. There's something hinky. I know it." Rey's hands gripped his shirt.

"Oh, honey." Mick rumbled softly, shaking his head. "You're just worrying because of the mate bond."

"So Dylan is having a bad feeling now?" Rey arched a brow at the boss. "I know what I know."

"Hey. Hey, we're professionals. We know what we're doing." Dylan reached out, stroked Rey's soft hair.

"I know! I'm a professional too, and I had a bad feeling about Elise and I went to her office anyway. Now she's dead." Rey grabbed his hand, holding on tight. "Dylan."

"Rey. You have to let us do this. This guy's an asshole and the police are already to move in. You'll be able to see everything on the monitors."

"You don't understand. Please. Listen to me. This is a mistake." Rey was just frantic.

"Rey." James shrugged when Dylan glanced at him. "I tried to tell him we all get nerves on the day of a sting or a hostage meet or whatever, but man, he was so serious."

"I'll be careful, sweetheart."

"Please, don't dismiss me. I'm not stupid or naive." Hadn't he proven his ability to read the vibrations with the crocs?

"I know that." Dylan raised his eyebrows, surprised at the statement. "I trust you. I do. But this is too hard to reschedule, and I need you safe. We need to settle this."

"I don't think it is going to be settled. I think... I think you're going to be sorry you've done this."

"Rey? Excuse us." Dylan took Rey by the arm, drawing him to the corner of the room. "What do you mean?" Surely Rey wasn't making a threat. He had to just be worried, but it was hard to read, he was so agitated.

He needed to understand.

"I don't know, mate. I don't. I feel like... I just feel it. Something's wrong. I can feel it. Everywhere."

"Are you sure it's not just because we're newly mated?" Dylan stroked up and down Rey's arms. "I don't want to make you mad, but this could take weeks to resolve if we don't go today. I know you have vibes, but we have to do this."

"It wasn't because we were mated yesterday. Yesterday it was because the crocs were here."

Dylan chewed his lip. Mick did believe they all had their talents. Maybe Rey was right.

He turned back to the rest of the pack. "He might be onto something. He had a feeling yesterday, just in time."

"So we'll be careful. Extra careful." Mick was growling. "We've got a big sting set up. We can't just blow it because of a feeling."

"Mick," Kit scolded. "Don't be a dick. We can do this, Rey. I get that dread thing, but we'll be careful."

"Please. I know this is wrong." Rey waved his hands, his frustration clear.

"Stop it, *raposo*. We'll take care of this for you, then you can find something else to keep Dylan busy." Brock's growl split the air. "Jesus, Dylan. Come on."

Dylan glared at Brock, but he knew they didn't have time for more arguing. He bent to kiss Rey on the lips. "Stay here. James will be on surveillance. He'll keep an eye out for us."

Rey nodded, shrinking under his kiss. "Be careful."

"Rey—" He didn't want to leave it like this.

"Dylan! Now." Mick had his Alpha voice on, and Dylan sighed, turning away from his mate. He would make it up to Rey later. They needed to get to the meet. Now.

Brock snarled something at Rey, and his mate just disappeared like a puff of smoke.

"Good one, Brock." Dylan got into Brock's space. "No messing with my mate. He was right yesterday."

"Yeah, and now we're forewarned. He's just confusing anxiety about you going into danger with some freakin' premonition." Brock rumbled softly. "He's a fox. He can't help it."

"What have you got against foxes again?" Dylan grabbed his sidearm, holstering it in the pancake holster at his back.

"Experience."

"Rey has done nothing but be kind to you!" Dylan barked.

"Guys, please." Kit was bright red. "Let's go to work?"

Mick growled in agreement. "You two can argue foxes later. Now we have a tiger to go after. No more distractions. Someone have the headsets?"

"Here. I'll get back upstairs." James handed over the comms, looking... strained. "Don't be too hard on the guy, Brock. He was really sick upstairs when the feeling hit him. Like pukey."

"If he's going to be having a conniption every time you have to work, he'll have to stay at your place, Dylan."

"Fine." His ears heated. Now he felt like no one was on his side. Not even his mate. "Can we go? I want to get this over with."

"Yeah, come on." Mick led the way, tucking the throat mic into place. Mick was armed to the teeth. The one thing he didn't have was the chip. That was in the safe. "Let's do this. I want this monkey off our backs."

Dylan nodded. He did too. He had a mate bond to finish cementing, and Rey was already pulling away.

"Let's go."

He'd explain later.

————

Rey went and packed all his things in his car, then he moved to clean the communal kitchen, straighten up the pantry and the meeting room. Then he went to James, just to see if everyone was okay.

He knew this was wrong. He knew it. He knew Dylan didn't care, and he knew that Brock wanted him out, gone before they got back, no matter how nice the man had been yesterday.

Okay, so. Right. He'd watch this, and then he'd go find an apartment close by so Dylan could visit sometimes.

"Rey? You okay, hon?" James gave him a small smile. Maybe a little embarrassed.

"Fine, thank you." He was sick and icy cold, and he knew something bad was coming, but he was just a fox. What did he know? "Are they there yet?"

"They're at the mall. Not in place yet." James patted the chair next to him.

He sat gingerly, nodding to James. "Sorry about this morning."

"What? Why? I get it. They didn't see you when it hit you. I think it's partly nerves, but I trust you."

That gave him a tiny burst of happiness, that James believed him.

The dread began to climb up his spine again, sliding up along into his brain. Nausea followed. Something was totally off.

"James. James, I don't feel so good."

"Shit." James caught him when he pitched over. "You're pale as milk."

"There's something co—" A shudder rocked the building, deep in its foundations.

James eased him back into the chair, then called up his cameras on the building. "What the fuck?"

Another shudder rolled through, and Rey cried out. "They're coming. They're coming for the SIM card."

"Run, Rey! The safe is in the basement in a strong room. Get down there. Lock yourself in." James grabbed a headset. "Mick! We're under attack!"

"On it. Stay safe."

Dylan had told him not to argue in an emergency, and he didn't want to distract James from his work. He ran downstairs as fast as he could, staying to the shadows. The crocs were here. Looking for them.

He would lock himself in and defend that stupid SIM card with his life. He'd been right, damn it, for all the good that did.

Rey made it to the main floor, and then scooted around to find the basement stairs. The building shook again, and one of the walls collapsed in on itself, the whole thing crumbling as if someone had set off a bomb.

"Oh my God." Rey was going to—well, he was running already, wasn't he, his feet and legs trying to tangle.

Downstairs. Downstairs. He didn't want to head down there. Not at all. Shit, the smell. Get the SIM card and get out. His head pounded, his nose full of the stink of croc.

A scaly, clawed hand caught the back of his neck, tearing at his skin, and he ducked down, ripping away.

He hit the stairs and slid down them on his ass. *Ow.* He managed to find his feet and run, ducking one of the crocs on the way. The huge fist came down, numbing his arm as he pushed by into the safe room.

Oh good gracious. What good was this safe room supposed to do him? He didn't have the combination to the safe. He tried to press the door closed, but something blew it back at him, and Rey went flying across the floor.

He slammed against the back of the wall, and the world went black.

———

"Mick! Mick, we're under attack!" James's voice came across their headsets, and Dylan felt a cold ball of dread form in the pit of his belly.

"*Merda!*" Brock's vicious curse was plain as day. "Get to the safe room, James!"

"I sent Rey. I need to keep everyone in the loop. They'll be after his scent, not mine."

A terrible sound came over the headsets, a desperate grinding that sounded like the screech of metal when a train derailed.

"I—The crocs are here, guys. Stay away, okay? Just stay safe." The bang and crash of some kind of explosion wiped out their comms, snuffing out James's voice, leaving nothing but feedback.

Dylan ripped off his headset. He was gonna… what? Puke? Cry? He ran toward where Mick was meant to meet Patel.

"Boss!"

There was a flash of light and he ducked and rolled, heading straight for Mick.

That smell hit him, the awful funk of stagnant water and reptile. "Down!" Dylan roared.

They rolled together, and he covered Mick, defending his Alpha with his own body.

Brock slid in next to them, turning his back to Dylan to provide cover fire if needed. Where the hell was Kit?

The big bear roared, the sound cracking through the air, then a broad, thick croc head went flying off into a nearby doorway.

Bear had shifted.

Dylan looked around, trying to assess the situation and finding only chaos.

"We need to retreat, Dylan. We have to get home." Brock's voice was a deep growl, his accent so heavy Dylan could barely make out the words.

"I know! Mick, you with us?" He hoped to hell Mick wasn't shot or something.

Another roar, another head. Wow. Kit's fury was glorious to behold. He'd seen some ultimate fighter thing once where a bear had so much pounds per pressure in a single swing or whatever, even a black bear and not a grizzly. Kit was proving it.

"With you. Have to get home." Mick was at about eighty-five percent growl.

"We should have stayed." Dylan might have snarled it, but he got Mick up, got him moving. He could hold a grudge later.

"Kit! Come on! We have to get James!" Mick shouted the words above the screams and grunts.

Kit roared, dropping to all fours to run in front of them. No one stood in his way, not cops, not crocs. They all dove for safety. Kit seemed larger than normal, kind of like the dire crocs had called out a dire bear.

Please, Dylan prayed, *let Rey be locked in the safe room*. Let his mate be whole and well. He'd never disregard his Rey's vibrations again. Never.

All they had to do was get back to the office. That was what he chose to believe.

They loaded Mick into the van, the big wolf still dazed. Brock was at the wheel. "Someone get Kit in here!"

Dylan whirled around, grabbing a big handful of fur. "In, bear! Now!"

Kit smelled awful, goo and gore dripping from him. His dark eyes were filled with rage, with raw fury.

Berserker.

Dylan shoved Kit over next to Mick, who was more than a little pale. "Are you hit, boss?"

"Just impact damage. That's it. We need to get to the HQ." Mick's voice was strong, at least.

"I'm working on it!" Brock gunned the engine, but something hit the back end of the van, spinning them part way around, the tires squealing.

"Go! Go! *Go!*" Fuck. His tiny mate was at the office with these fuckers!

Brock floored it and they burned out, the sound of sirens blaring as they left the lot. Good. The local LEOs could do cleanup.

"Dylan, my phone," Brock shouted. "I can call in some backup. I know some guys."

"Are they 'shoot the fox on sight' people like you?" he snarled.

"Stop it! I...."

"Enough!" Mick snapped.

Dylan shook it off. "I won't apologize, but it's not doing any good." He found the phone. "Who am I calling?"

"Just pair it with the van."

"On it." He paired the phone, trying not to short out with worry.

Brock made the call, the name unfamiliar. "Call Griz." When a gruff voice answered, Brock hailed the guy. "Hey, *homem*, I need back up at my office location. Croc shifter attack. We were drawn off site, but our communications man and our client are there. Fox and mountain lion. Thanks." Brock ended the call. "Help on the way."

"Thank you." He would beat Brock down after Rey and James were safe.

Hell, at this rate, Brock would let him, he'd bet. To a point.

Kit sat on the floor of the van, naked and shivering. "My bag, boss?"

"You got it, kiddo." Mick handed over the backpack.

"Rey and James? Have you heard from them?"

"No. Not since the attack." Worry ate at Dylan, but he knew he had to channel it into efficient, cool-headed rage.

"Now we know that Kit knows how to deal with the crocs, it'll be easy," Mick teased.

Kit snorted. "Was it bad? I mean, I cut a swath."

"You did fine, Kit." Dylan had been impressed. Damn impressed. Bear-3. Crocs-0.

"Thanks. I guess I do know what to do, then." Kit's smile was strained.

"Yeah, and I just called in another bear and whoever he has available to help."

"No shit." Mick looked to the driver's seat. "Damn."

"Griz is amazing. Old friend."

Dylan looked at Brock too, stunned. "You have friends?"

Brock bared his teeth without taking his eyes off the road. "I do. I said I was sorry."

"Did you?" Dylan sighed. "We should have listened. I'll never forgive myself if—"

"You'd know if he was... well, you'd know. You're mates. He'll be fine."

"If he ever forgives me," Dylan rumbled, distressed.

Kit touched his arm. "He's a good guy. You'll work it out."

"I will." He had to. Dylan loved Rey too much not to.

And he would apologize all over himself, grovel, and promise to never do it again.

Rey had been right. Something terrible had happened and they shouldn't have left.

Brock took a corner on two wheels, tossing Dylan against the seat. "Ooooph."

"Just trying to get us there."

"Uh-huh. You just want me broken and bruised.'"

"You know it. My life is infinitely better when you guys are all broken up." That kitty lip curled.

God, he wished Brock could just... breathe. Stop taking everything so personally.

They rounded the final corner that led to the lot of their building and—

Oh Christ, the place was gonna fall down.

Mick gawked. "Motherfucker."

"We need to.... Mick, James and Rey are in here." Kit sounded broken.

"We'll get them out." Mick sounded pissed now rather than weak. That was good. Pissed-off Mick was the superior wolf. "Sniff them out, Kit. Brock, we need that backup now."

"Their ETA's two minutes." Brock slid them into the lot at their building like a baseman rounding third and going for home.

"Got it. You keep watch. I'm going around. Dylan, keep Kit's back."

"James said Rey went to the safe room in the basement. I'm going to fuzz out again, Dylan. I can smell better that way."

"Okay, try to stay in there for me, though. Think human."

"I'll try."

Kit could lose his manly side a bit.

They headed into the destroyed building, Kit's unhappy growls getting louder and louder.

"Kit. Come on, man, we need Rey and James. Our pack. Our den."

Smoke and sparks were on the air, and the fire department would come soon. Dammit. Then Dylan saw a golden paw dangling in the rubble.

"James!" Dylan loped over the mess, hoping Kit was finding his mate. He lifted sheetrock off James's mountain lion form. James was unconscious, but his chest was moving, drawing shaky breaths.

Dylan had to dare to move him. The rest of the building could come down any time. "I'm going to move you, James. No biting. Wake up, huh? Let me see your eyes?" James lifted his head slightly, golden eyes barely slitted open. "It's me, Dylan. I'll take you to Brock, but I have to find Rey."

He needed his mate. Whole and hale and hearty.

There was nothing on that front. Absolutely nothing.

Rey wasn't dead. He knew it. He couldn't bear it if Rey was gone after only a couple of days. Everyone said he would know too. So what was this? Was Rey unconscious?

Kit came to him, big head swinging side to side.

"What, man? Let me get James out." The cat was viciously heavy.

Kit nudged him, making this awful noise, and for a terrible

moment he thought Kit had found Rey. Then he realized what the headshake meant. Kit hadn't.

"He's not here? Kit? You can't find him?"

Kit moaned, the sound mournful. He shook his head again.

"We have to get James help. Then I have to find him. What about the safe?" He headed back toward the van, picking his way carefully.

Kit disappeared with a roar, heading back into the mess.

"Brock. James is hurt bad." He laid James on the floor of the van.

Brock growled softly. "You found your mate?"

"No. Kit thinks he's not here. I have to find him." Dylan would take one of the company cars and head for... the mansion they'd seen on the video, maybe.

"What about the safe?" Mick asked. "Did they get that?"

Dylan understood the question. He did. If they had the SIM card, there was no reason to keep Rey alive.

"Kit is looking."

A roar sounded, and Mick ran off again. A few moments later they heard Mick shouting, "It's here!"

"Okay. Okay, we have to get hold of the fucker and make the swap," Dylan snapped. "You know they have Rey."

A big SUV squealed up, two burly types popping out. "Brock. What do you need?" asked one of the men.

"Dylan's mate has been taken, guys. Dylan, this is Grizzly Locke and... and friend," Brock finished when the other big guy never said a word.

"Thanks for coming, guys. I need to find my mate." He headed for the back parking.

Mick jogged back to him. "No. You need to drive the van while I call and make the meet."

"But...."

"I will help you get him back, Dylan. You have my word."

"I think I might just die, Mick." His whole body felt heavy, his head pounding. Knowing Rey was taken by those... things made him sick and worried.

"No. We need you. Rey needs you."

"He needs all of us. Promise me."

"Pack. He's pack. You have my word."

"Thank you." He climbed into the van, right into the driver's seat. Kit would have to patch up James if he could, and Brock would be coordinating with his new guys. He felt old. Decrepit. His joints hurt as if he was trying to shift back before Rey came along.

"Buck up, Dylan. We'll get him. He's got to be wigged as hell."

"If he's conscious. There's just this hole where he ought to be. What if they're hurting him?"

Kit grunted, the man emerging from the bear as he climbed into the van. He pulled on clothes before kneeling by James. "Hey, buddy. I'm touching, so no biting."

Dylan snorted, because that was what he'd said.

James chuffed softly, staring up at him with dazed eyes.

"Hey, bud. You know Kit. He's got to find where you're hurt so he can fix it."

He knew Mick had to get the safe open, but he had to move. To search.

James sighed, and Mick worked the safe. "Got it. Got the SIM card. Let's make the trade."

Dylan nodded. "Let's go."

"Brock, your guys need to be on our heels." Mick was back on even ground, it seemed, ready to work.

"We're moving. Do you know where we're going?" Brock headed to the vehicle the new guys had arrived in.

Dylan frowned, trying to catch a thought he'd had earlier, and then jerked like lightning had hit him. The pool. That pool. "The house Rey found."

"The one up by the gardens? Got it."

"We're on your ass," Brock said.

Dylan nodded, closing the driver's door while Mick closed the van's slider.

"Go, go, go," Mick said, then tugged out his phone to call the tiger, Dylan assumed.

I'm coming, Rey. He was. He was getting his mate and....

Well, he didn't have an *and*.

All he could do was get there fast and kick some croc ass. His mate was not bait. Not a commodity.

"Patel," Mick barked. "Your methods suck. I have the SIM card. Where's our fox?"

Dylan hated that he couldn't hear the other end of the conversation.

"Don't you fuck with me, man. You lost a few crocs already." Mick said it with savage satisfaction.

Dylan turned off on the highway, knowing he could gun it that way. He wasn't willing to sit at red lights.

Mick snarled. "You touch him, I'll let our bear eat you."

They had two bears now. And another huge guy who could surely rip off croc heads. "I'll eat his fucking eyes out," Dylan murmured.

"We'll be there." Mick said, then hung up. "He wants to meet us at the gardens. I think we'll just run him down at the house. It's a rental and a marvel of modern architecture. Even a guy like him won't want it destroyed."

"I don't care if I have to tear it down with my bare hands," Dylan spat out.

Mick nodded, baring his teeth. "We take Rey, we keep the SIM card, and we get the hell out."

"Got it." Kit growled. "James is down for the fight. We'll have to make sure he's secure."

"He's going to make it?" Mick asked.

"Yeah, but his body is using all its energy now to heal. He has some crush injuries and one bad head bump."

Mick's rumble didn't bode well for the tiger man. Not at all.

"How are you, Kit?"

"Ready to get Rey back. Where are we going to go, Mick? They ruined our home." Kit's soft agony was so clear.

"We'll get something even better. Something that even Dylan will stay with us at, huh?" Mick winked at him from across the way.

Dylan grunted. Yeah, having James and Rey there had worked out so well.

"All my Doctor Who stuff...." Kit sighed.

"We'll fix it, Kit. Believe. First this."

"Rey," Dylan snapped. "First Rey."

"There's time for my 'I'm sorries' later, Dylan. And I will." Mick was always willing to own up to when he was wrong; he had to give the man that. He was a good Alpha.

"I just need him back in my arms, Mick."

"We're almost there. We're going in hot."

Dylan nodded, checking the rearview. Brock was right on their six, riding his bumper. They weren't going in alone at all. The new guys were a bit of a wild card, something Patel wouldn't expect.

Then they had their own bear, Brock's friends, and Dylan's own personal rage. Kit was awesome in his rampage mode. They would run this tiger to ground, and they wouldn't stop until they had him beaten.

Suddenly he heard a scream, a wild noise echoing between his ears.

Relief made his hands shake on the wheel. Rey was alive. Alive and able to reach out to him.

"I can hear him, guys. Rey. He says Patel is batshit crazy. Like, totally lost his shit."

"Goodie. Someone tell me James made backups of the SIM card."

"Three." Kit shrugged when they all stared at him. "He sent one to the cloud, made one on a hard copy, and had one saved locally. So we should have the one on the cloud even if we've lost all the hard drives from upstairs."

"How do you know?"

"I was upstairs talking to James." Kit rolled his eyes. "I do visit with people, you know."

"Shut up." The refrain from Mick was fond. "Okay, good. We have leverage."

"Leverage and guns." Dylan was all over the "I'm pissed and I'm armed" approach.

"Yeah. Well, he might be well-armed too."

"I don't think so, boss," Kit said. "Those crocs are his weapons. Maybe it's hard for him to get because he's a foreign national, but ammo doesn't seem to be his thing."

"Still, none of us are armor-plated. You hear me, bear?" Mick growled.

"I got it." Kit stroked James's ears. "Hang in there, buddy."

James turned his head, teeth gently grasping Kit's wrist.

"That's it." Kit sounded tickled that James was that mobile. Dylan didn't blame him one bit.

"Lock and load," Dylan said, pulling off at the exit closest to the mansion Patel was renting.

"I won't leave your mate behind, Dylan," Mick growled.

"No. That's not an option." No one was going to get out of there until he got Rey.

Not even close.

Rey focused on staying perfectly still and pretending to be unconscious.

"...tell those idiots that I will buy them out, no question. I will take the company and leave them sobbing in their nappies!"

Was that even how it worked? Gracious, Rey didn't know. He didn't care. He wanted to be out of here and with Dylan, away from the craziness.

He was in fox form, trapped in a little wire cage, a croc draped over the top of him.

The stink was... unbearable.

He knew Dylan could hear him, and that gave him hope. Was James okay? He had a feeling not. The building had fallen on him. Well, parts of it, at any rate, and that was never well-done.

The crocs had taken Rey, beaten the snot out of him—rather gently for a croc, he thought—then thrown him in here. Obviously he didn't have the damn SIM card, now did he? So why were they waiting? Why hadn't they taken James, who was important to the team?

The tiger stalked up, swatting at the cage and the croc with it. Rey rolled and went with the motion. He didn't need any more bruises. He could stand it if the cage popped open, though, so he could run.

"God!" Patel kicked the croc. "We need to go kill this wolf and his pack. Do you understand?"

Dylan's voice came to him at the same time he heard the hum of an engine approaching outside. *We're coming, mate.*

Yes. Oh yes, that would be lovely.

There was grim determination in Dylan's mental voice. And rage.

Please.

He didn't want to die here. Not like this.

Rey tensed, ready to bolt. The croc yawned, huge teeth showing, then snapping idly at the tiger man.

The man swung his hand down, and the croc moved away,

the fist slamming into the cage, shattering it. That was all Rey needed and he was off and running, his tail like a rudder behind him.

He could outrun a croc and a tiger, at least in the short-term, clocking almost thirty miles an hour at full speed.

"Get him!" Patel roared.

The sound of gunshots outside might have deterred him if he didn't need to get out of the house so much.

He zoomed to the stairs, staying low as he hid in the dark shadows. Okay. Okay, he had to go up. He had to....

Two bears barreled down the stairs—one familiar black bear and the biggest grizzly he'd ever seen. Goodness. Was that.... He thought the black bear was Kit. Maybe.

He didn't want to get eaten, by croc or by bear.

Crocs went flying, the bears working together like Viking warriors on a raid. He shook his head, taking another step, another.

There was some strain across the mate bond he could feel, as if Dylan was in fight mode.

He had to trust that the bears would—

A huge hand grabbed him, shook him so hard that the world shuddered, went black and sparkly about the edges.

Oh God. This was it. Patel was going to kill him.

A snarl sounded, and a large gray wolf flew down the last few steps in a tremendous leap, hitting Patel right at waist level. He bit and tore, going for maximum damage. He wasn't as big as Patel, but he had lots of teeth.

"Fuck!" the big man roared, staggering back and dropping him. Dylan leaped in, attacking Patel at the Achilles. All the roars and blood and pain were making Rey dizzy, making him crazed enough that he ran in circles.

Dylan put himself between Rey and Patel, pushing him back toward the stairs.

Patel shifted halfway, claws slashing through the air.

Dylan leaped back, growling and snapping. Rey knew he was meant to go upstairs, but he couldn't let Dylan face this alone. Now, now he knew what to do.

Rey climbed up the outstretched arm, going for an eye, an ear. He had serrated canines; he could help.

The tiger man growled, beating at him, and he flew. One of the bears caught him, surprising a sharp sound out of him when he didn't hit the wall.

He barked, and then Dylan went in for the attack again, teeth flashing. The tiger tossed him, and Dylan slammed into the brick wall, a yelp of pain sounding. Rey felt the pain slamming through his mate.

Rey scrambled, trying to get to Dylan.

Patel stalked over toward Dylan, claws out, a wild roar on the air. Rey couldn't reach his mate in time; he couldn't get there, so he did what he could.

He screamed, the sound piercing the air and stilling everything. Time stopped, both bears and crocs frozen, staring at him. Dylan only paused a moment, then rose to all four paws to lope past Patel.

Dylan scooped Rey up in his jaws and ran, drawing them up the stairs.

Brock met them at the top, armed to the teeth. "Van! Go!"

Dylan didn't hesitate and they were flying, heading right for the van. He clung to Dylan, his claws in Dylan's ruff. He could retract them, but not now.

He wasn't sure if he was rejoicing or losing his ever-loving mind.

Dylan leapt into the van, the impact shuddering through them. Bruised and sore and scared, but fine. They were both fine, and Rey could hardly believe they were alive.

Brock slid into the driver's seat. "My guys will get Kit and Mick. We got to go. Get the fox and James safe."

He growled softly, his lip jerking up. He and Brock weren't friends. Not at all. Not friends.

Brock ignored him, and Dylan started grooming him as they got rolling, Brock speeding toward the gate.

He sighed as the soreness began to grow, the deep ache filling him.

Dylan nosed him.

He'd done his best to help, but....

James lay on the floor of the van, pillows and blankets supporting him. He was in cat form, but there was blood.

Rey crawled toward the big cat, guilt tearing at him. He'd left James to run to the safe room.

One golden eye opened, focusing on him, and James made a sweet, happy noise. Oh, so dear.

He rubbed their muzzles together, terribly careful not to hurt.

James sighed, head resting back down on the—

Something hit the van like a battering ram just as they were about to slide through the gate.

Oh no! He turned, stumbling as Brock fought to keep the van on the road. They swung in a sickening, low circle, then the thing hit them again, and the van went over like a Tonka toy.

He shifted to human so he could wrap around James, hold on tight to his wounded friend.

Dylan barked sharply, lunging out the bent, open passenger door after Brock, who had flown out when the door popped awry.

Rey grabbed the shotgun that was between the seats. "Okay, James. I'm getting fucking tired of this."

James snarled, those big feet flexing as he tried to get up.

"Stay down. I'm naked with a gun and being chased by a livid tiger. I'm sure I'm going to need you to have my back."

Rey hopped out of the van to a scene of utter chaos. The

grizzly was chasing down a croc, which was fascinating and gross when the bear ripped out the croc's spine.

Dylan and Mick were grappling with Patel, and Rey knew there was no way. No way.

Tigers were the biggest of the big cats. They could kill a pack of wolves if they needed to. "Dylan! Down!" A shotgun would do some damage. Enough to take Patel down, if not kill him.

Rey didn't hesitate, and he didn't spout a monologue. He just shot, hitting Patel in the shoulder.

Dylan whirled back to Patel, going for the legs while Mick went for the throat. They worked seamlessly like the pack they were, even as sirens and lights began to fill the air, even as Patel began to sink down.

He figured the fight was all over when the grizzly bear came and sat on Patel, holding him. Kit lumbered up, nose working hard. Rey slipped back in the van and put the weapon away before checking on James.

James was panting, that pink tongue hanging out, the golden eyes open to slits. He'd managed to crawl to the open door but was stuck there, half in and half out.

"Kit! Kit, I need help!"

Rey didn't want to hurt anyone, but Kit didn't seem worried at all. Kit just swooped in and scooped James right up.

There was another vehicle, one the other bear was now pulling clothes out of.

"This has been the weirdest day ever." Rey sat down on the seat, talking to no one at all, beginning to shake.

"Hey, you must be Rey," the guy who had just been a bear said, bringing him a pair of sweats and a T-shirt. "They said you were small, so I got a medium. I'm Locke. The cops are coming."

"Okay. What is the plan?" What did you do when you shot a mean tiger and all the bears had crocodile goo on them?

"The plan is for all of us but Mick to get out of here. He'll hand Patel over to the police, who will hold him until whatever government agency wants him comes to get him. He'll get maximum security. Brock says Dylan still has some friends on the force."

"Okay." So he was... done. The case was over. "I guess Mick will bill me."

He put his clothes on—no, he put on some hand-me-downs.

Gracious. Was he liable for Mick's building? He didn't have that much in savings. At all. He wasn't sure he could cover the van....

Dylan snuffled at him, clearly having a hard time shifting. He reached out, immediately, cradling Dylan's muzzle in his hands.

Dylan was warm, heavy, damp in a few places. Rey hoped it wasn't blood.

"Are you hurt? I have you. I have you, mate." He stroked and petted, drawing the man out.

Dylan panted, then that big wolf body strained.

He rested his forehead against Dylan's, urging Dylan to be all right.

Dylan shuddered again, then he backed away, the wolf becoming the man.

"There you are." Rey grabbed a blanket and wrapped it around Dylan.

"Here I am." Dylan's voice was rough, his face all bruised. "Are you okay?"

"Uh-huh." Rey shook his head side to side. He was scared and bruised and lost and he didn't know what to do.

"Hey. Hey, come here." People were moving around them, Kit holding James, the Locke guy getting the wheels going, leaving Mick and Brock and the overturned van.

Dylan held him, wrapped up in the blanket with him. Rey

stayed close and still, totally unsure about what happened next.

"Shhh." Dylan stroked his back. "There's a lot to be figured out. My place has a few empty apartments. I bet Mick will rent a few just until he figures out what to do next."

"I'm going to owe you guys forever." Maybe longer.

"For what?" Dylan sounded genuinely bewildered.

"Everything that's broken."

"We have insurance. Hell, the building carries enough to rebuild it twice." Dylan nuzzled him. "You're one of us, baby. Pack."

"No one believed me." Rey probably needed to get over it, but James had almost died and Dylan was all bruised and....

"I'll never doubt you again," Dylan said.

"Me either." That came from Kit. "Not ever."

"It's not about you. I mean, it is, but not because of your job. I know when things are wrong."

"I get that now, sweetheart. I let Brock and Mick sway me." Dylan hung his head.

"Brock wants me to leave. To stay away." The fierceness of Brock's growls had surprised him. He'd given the man hugs!

"Brock's hurt, Rey. Please forgive him." Kit sounded so wrecked, so sincere. "I think he knows you're good. He let you love on him. He just had such a bad thing."

Dylan nodded. "We don't know exactly the whole story, but it had to be bad." Dylan nudged him. "You don't have to. I'll respect it. But...."

"Stop it. We have a thousand things to deal with first. Like James."

"Right. Uh. Who's driving?"

"Brock's friend Grizzly Locke. Brock and Locke." Kit started laughing, the sound a little hysterical.

He reached out, took Kit's hand. "Breathe, bear."

"Sorry." Kit's laughter faded to chuckles as he sucked in air.

"So, Locke?" Dylan raised his voice to be heard. "Where are we going?"

"Brock has a house in Aurora."

"No shit?" Dylan's eyebrows rose to his hairline.

"No shit. It's... significant and safe, if I recall correctly. It's been a while."

"Wow. Okay." Dylan chuckled. "The things we don't know."

"He knows to meet us there."

"That's cool. We need to get cleanup crews at the building too."

"I'll go do it," Rey offered.

"No, you won't," Dylan growled. "You will stay with me." The hand that wrapped around his hip was sure and firm.

"I will, will I?"

"Yes. I made that mistake once." Dylan snorted. "I mean, we can't be together 24/7, but when you have a feeling...."

"You'll need time for the bond to finish cementing," Locke said. "You both know that, right?"

"What does that mean?" Kit asked.

"Mates form a bond—it's chemical at first, but the emotional part will come, the sexual part."

"Oh, they have the sex part down," Kit teased.

"Kit!" Rey flushed.

"Well, we do." Dylan laughed, his voice more normal.

"We could still practice a little more," Rey pointed out.

"I think that's a fine idea."

"Not now, please," Locke said.

"No, that would be awkward," Rey agreed.

"Gross," Kit pointed out.

"Possibly even nasty." That was Locke.

"Maybe hot as hell." Dylan winked down at him.

"Maybe?" He was going to have to work harder if *maybe* was the best he got.

"Definitely."

"Oh God. James, help me." Kit rolled his eyes, but he was laughing again. "Does anyone have a phone? I think mine is in the van."

"Mine too," Dylan said. "In fact, I think, except for Locke, we're all phoneless."

Kit gasped. "I'm not sure I can survive."

"Don't worry, guys." Locke tossed back a flip unit. "Burn phone."

"Oh, my precious...." Kit grabbed it, stroking it like a pet.

Rey began to laugh, the sound starting low and filling the air.

Kit winked at him. "I'll call Mick, see how it's going?"

"Yeah, we all need to be together." Dylan sighed. "Much as I always hate to admit it."

Kit tapped out a number. "Hey, boss. Yeah, we're going to —did you know Brock had a house? Uh-huh. Okay. See you there."

Dylan tugged him in closer, resting his head on that broad chest.

Rey sighed. He felt as if everything was still up in the air, but he did know one thing. This was his mate, and he was going to look forward to all the parts of the bond.

TEN

Every bit of Dylan hurt. Well, his heart was feeling better knowing Rey was going to forgive him. Or had, as long as he didn't make that same mistake again.

Brock's house was... wow. Easily a million-dollar beauty. There was so much new construction in the area, but this place had five acres, a ton of wood and stone detail, and a four-car garage.

Really? Mr. Kitty was keeping this from them? Them?

He shook his head, but he was incredibly grateful there was a place for them to regroup.

"Hey, *amigos*." Brock swept into the amazing leather-couched den and game room where Locke had taken them and set up triage for Kit and James.

"Hey, Brock. Nice house," Dylan teased.

"Thanks. There's room for everyone. I'll even let you and Rey share."

"Gee, you're a prince." Dylan made a face, which caused Brock to laugh.

"Does someone have a line on Carrie?" Dylan asked.

"We do. One of Locke's guys is at her mom's standing guard."

"Mick, how did it go with the cops?" Dylan asked.

"They asked us to head out and come in individually in a day or so. They wanted to keep the shifter element as quiet as possible, and they already had a couple of dead crocs to explain."

"We'll start with the cleanup soon, too. I want to see what we can save." Dylan hated that Mick's building was down and out.

"I'll help," Rey murmured. "I feel so guilty."

Dylan opened his mouth to protest, but Mick fixed Rey with a stern glare. "Nonsense. You hired us to do a job and we fucked up. We should have listened to you."

"I—" Rey stopped protesting, then shrugged. "Thanks, Mick. I swear, I was telling the truth. I'll never just give warning for no reason."

"I may be pigheaded, but I'll trust you from now on."

Brock snorted, and Dylan glared at him until he flushed. "Okay, I was wrong, okay? I'm sorry. I really am, Rey. No one needed to get hurt like this."

"No. No, none of us did." Rey met Brock's gaze. "Not any of us."

"No." Brock looked at James, who was sedated and sleeping a healing sleep. "God." He turned his back, but they all saw the expression that pulled at his face.

Rey sighed softly, then stood and went to Brock, giving the big bastard a hug.

Mick stared at them, then at him. "He's a good guy."

"Yeah, he is." Dylan was so proud. "What about Patel?"

"Started screaming. Foaming. Monologued about killing Rey's client because she was going to take the SIM card to the press and make a big thing."

"He killed her? For that?" Dylan shook his head, but he felt Rey's dull horror.

"He did. I'm sorry, Rey. Just remember, you didn't do anything. The guy is a nutburger." Mick just shook his head in patent amazement.

"Oh my goodness." Rey shook his head. "She was a nice lady trying to get a job."

"I'm sorry, Rey. Criminals like that...." Kit made a face too, a huge grimace.

Brock turned and gave Rey a hug back. "Sorry, *doce*."

Rey looked panicked, utterly freaked, and Dylan vocalized softly, opening his arms. His mate disengaged from Brock and flew to him, hiding away with a soft noise. Poor love.

Dylan held Rey, rocking him.

"You guys need to go crash. Alone," Kit said softly.

"Yeah, come on, I'll show you a room," Brock agreed.

"Thanks, man." Dylan scooped Rey up under his arm. "Lead on."

Brock led them upstairs, down the hall to the second room to the end on the right. The place had a seating area, a mini wet bar, and the bed on a platform at the end of the room.

"Spiffy." Dylan approved. "Thanks, man. We appreciate it."

"No problem. Yell if you need anything. There's a house phone, and Griz will have someone monitoring it. Dial nine."

"Dial nine. Rock on." Dylan put Rey on the bed and followed Brock to the door, sparing a moment to wonder what Grizzly Locke and Brock had to do with one another. Probably none of his business. "Thanks, man."

"*Não tem problema.*"

Dylan shut the door behind Brock and locked it. He loved the guys, but the rest of today was his and Rey's to rest up, to be together. "Hey, there's even a bathroom in here. Wow."

"With a shower?" Rey sounded so needy.

"Yes. God, yes." He went to pick Rey back up, plucking him easily off the bed.

"I-I feel so...."

"Shh. Shh, I know. Let's get warm and clean, okay? That'll help."

"I hurt. The croc laid over top of my cage. Stinky."

"I know. He hit me and I thought he'd broken me in two. The tiger, not the croc." Dylan shook his head. "When you screamed, the world stopped."

"I— We can do that. Foxes. It's actually a mating call."

"It was perfect." Dylan got the water running, the steam starting almost immediately. That was a good water heater. "Imagine Brock having this place and none of us knowing. I wonder if he rents it out."

"I wonder if he hates having all of us here."

"It didn't look like it. I mean, he lives at the office. Has an apartment." Dylan was a little wigged out at how much he didn't know about one of their team members. "Let's get these sweats off you."

"We can ask. Later." Rey was covered in bruises, just covered.

"Sure. I'll make a note." Dylan stripped off the rest of their borrowed clothes.

"Dear Brock, WTF? Love, Us."

Dylan laughed, delighted at Rey's snark. "Right? We ask that a lot around Apex." Dylan pulled Rey under the hot water, the spray almost unbearable it felt so good. He held Rey, cradling his lover, keeping him close.

"The water is so nice." Rey's voice was muffled against his chest.

"Yeah. Is it helping?"

"You're helping, Dylan."

"Good." He wanted to help. His mate had been

kidnapped by a homicidal tiger. Laid on by crocodiles. He wanted to go kill something, even though he knew Patel was more valuable alive and also contained now.

"I need you to love me, not kill something."

"I will, then." Dylan damned the bruises and went full speed ahead, taking the kiss he so desperately needed.

Rey pushed up to kiss him back, the lean body shivering and shaking against him.

He wanted to comfort, but he also needed. He was ragingly hard, his desire for Rey very real and immediate.

Rey's hand wrapped around his hardness, stroking him from base to tip, nudging the slit.

"Oh fuck." Dylan swayed, his hips punching forward.

"Uh-huh." Rey hummed and stroked again, petting him.

"Rey."

Rey beamed at him, moaning softly as he lifted his face for a kiss.

Dylan took it, and they rocked and rubbed. He hadn't expected this sudden need, this absolute desire to affirm life. He wanted to fill Rey up, make his mate scream for him.

Oh, that was promising. Anything was always a good thing. Well, when it came to sex with his mate. He lifted Rey up, and Rey climbed him like a challenging tree.

"Ride me? Right here like this?"

"Goddess, yes. Right here, like this." Rey nodded hard, water flying.

Thank God Brock was a prepared man. This bathroom had more slick stuff in the shower than any pleasure palace. He was going to have to remember to do this. Seriously. Dylan wasn't a single wolf anymore.

Dylan grabbed a tube that looked new from among the bottles of conditioner and skin cream, then popped it open. He didn't have time to wait.

He needed to touch Rey, to mark him, deep inside.

Dylan got his fingers slick, Rey holding himself up so Dylan had his hands free. Then he slid two of them around behind Rey, pressing them where he wanted his cock to be soon. Rey's eyes lit up, his mate's lips parting.

"Mmm-hmm. Hot. So hot inside." He pushed his fingers deeper, moving back and forth.

Rey stared at him, eyes wide, tongue flicking out to wet his lips.

"Sweet fox." He hummed, working his fingers in and out, loving how Rey's body gripped him.

"Yours. Yours. Harder, Dylan. More."

"More," he agreed. He pulled his fingers free, ready to give Rey his cock. "Want you to ride me, Rey. Now."

"Now." Rey lifted up a little higher, arching his back.

"Fuck." He grabbed his cock, guiding it to Rey's hole, and Rey pushed down, taking him to the root in one steady motion.

Dylan braced himself, and Rey grabbed the showerhead for leverage. They began to move together, slow at first, then faster.

He looked down, watching Rey's body ripple, watching the hard prick slide on his belly. That was the prettiest thing ever, all that red hair and flushed skin. His beautiful mate.

"Oh...."

Yes. Back and forth, the feelings rebounded between them, growing with every moment. It was a maddening echo, reverberating between them, over and over, the sound getting louder by the second.

Dylan closed his eyes and leaned against the cold tile wall, trying to get his bearings. Rey reached up, cupped Dylan's face, and the world came into sharp focus.

His eyes flew open and he stared into Rey's copper gaze. Caught. Right there.

Rey's ass fluttered around him, milking him, gripping his prick.

"Rey!" Dylan danced, his cock jerking madly. He was going to short right out.

That needy plea had him rocking hard, driving into his lover. Rey was begging him, asking him for release, so Dylan drove toward it, panting, his muscles tight even under the hot water. Soon. Soon.

Rey nodded, answering the warning he didn't give voice to.

He grunted when Rey squeezed down on him, clamping down like a heated vise. That was all it took for Dylan to growl, his body giving up the goods, his seed filling Rey deep.

Dylan jacked Rey, hand moving hard and fast, even as he buzzed with his own orgasm. He needed Rey with him in all ways. "Come on, sweetheart. Come for me. Come on." He pushed Rey a little along their bond too.

Rey grunted, his entire body jerking forward. His fox squeezed tight around his prick, jerking around him as Rey shot.

Dylan hummed, the sound proud and satisfied. Yeah. Damn. The water was still hot too. Good water heater.

Rey moaned for him, hanging on him like a limpet.

"Come on, sweetheart. There's a big bed. Not a cot."

"What'll we do with all that space?" Rey teased.

"Stretch out. I'm usually a sprawler." If there was a window, he was so letting in the sun too. They were safe up here on the second floor with their whole crew downstairs.

"Not me. I always end up curled into a ball."

"Well, we just have to make sure you have lots of pillows." He felt better. Less bruised and looser in his skin.

"Or my mate."

"You can totally curl up on me." He turned off the water, then got towels. Time to hold each other and rest.

Rey helped, drying him off. Oh, he hadn't ever enjoyed a simple shower so much.

They walked hand in hand to the bed, then crawled in under the blankets to make a cocoon. He drew Rey in close, petting him carefully.

He wouldn't let go until he had to.

———

Rey woke in the middle of the night, adrenaline rushing through him, driving him up in the mattress, his heart pounding.

"Rey?" Dylan was right there, hand on his arm, voice rough with sleep.

"Bad dream. Been a weird day."

"Just a little, yeah." Dylan's belly rumbled, and he felt as much as heard it.

"Hungry wolf." He started to laugh, the chuckles bubbling out of him. Dylan was always hungry.

"I am! I swear, action makes me empty. Shifting takes it out of me too. It's easier with you, though." Dylan stroked his cheek.

"I'm glad. I want things to be easy, you know? Just normal, easy." He looked over, waggled his eyebrows, and winked. "Holler if you figure out how to make that happen."

"I will. I mean, we did meet under kinda extreme circumstances. Usually my job is dull. Really dull."

"Mine too. I guess." Except he was going to have to start from scratch now.... Many of his contacts were dead, and the rest would have heard through the grapevine by now and wouldn't answer when he called.

No one would trust an information broker and courier who'd gone and gotten a client killed.

"Mmm. We'll see." Dylan took his hand and kissed it. "I'm keeping you. You know that, right? You're my mate."

"I know." That much he didn't question anymore, but they still had to really get to know each other. Also, what he was going to do to contribute? Gracious, that worried him.

"Shh. Rey. I have you."

"Thank you. I'm sorry. I didn't mean to wake you."

"No, I know. Do you mind if we get a snack?" Dylan stroked his leg.

His belly snarled right back. "Please? Something tasty?"

"Yep. I would bet Kit has a million choices down in the kitchen by now. That bear has an unnatural love for Walmart." Dylan rose, lifting Rey out of the bed. "In fact, I bet...." He strode to the door and opened it to find three bags outside their door. "Clothes."

"Wow. You guys take care of each other, don't you?" The entire dynamic of Apex Investigations fascinated him; he'd been such a loner in his adult life.

"We do. I swear, you're one of us. Sometimes it takes a while to grease all the wheels." Dylan tugged on a T-shirt that said "Rub me the right way" with a corgi butt facing out.

Rey stared and started to laugh again. Oh, what had they picked for him?

"Let me see?" Dylan asked.

Rey help up a unicorn shirt that said "Don't make me stab you with my head."

"Sheer perfection." He put it on, along with the soft shorts. He probably looked like a dork, but he was comfortable. Kit was good to him, which was so sweet, since he was the new guy.

Dylan took his hand. "Barefoot okay?"

"Of course." He felt weirdly comfortable, as if he were welcome here.

They went hand in hand down the stairs and through the

great room to the kitchen. Soft lighting was still on through-out, letting anyone unfamiliar with the house wander, Rey guessed.

"This is amazing. How neat that Brock has a hidey-hole." A hidey-mansion?

"I think so, yeah. I would bet this place was a fallback in case of something just like this." Dylan shrugged. "Oh, something smells good."

Rey sniffed, nostrils flaring. "Oh, you're right."

When they hit the kitchen, Kit was there, mixing something in a giant stoneware bowl. He glanced up, a sheepish look on his face. "I couldn't sleep."

Pans lay all over the granite counters, covered with towels.

"Can I help?" Rey went to Kit and hugged him tight. "Hey, bear."

"Um, the two loaves on top of the stove need to go in the bottom oven. I already have it at temp." Kit lifted Rey clean off the floor to hug him back. "I'm so glad you're okay."

"Me too. So glad to be... whole. I hear you were a stud, man."

"I don't remember much. I can lose myself a little when I'm mad. Bear Hulk." Kit chuckled. "Made me want to make bread, though."

Dylan put the two loaves in the oven, grinning at them. "Well, it smells amazing."

"Thanks. There's a cake, some turkey sandwiches, peanut butter. Cinnamon raisin bread for you, Rey."

"Oh." He clapped his hands. "Thank you."

"Peanut butter?" Dylan asked.

"In cookies and for the bread."

"Uhn. Cookies." Rey pounced. He was starving again. Man, he was glad he was shifting and running and scared and stuff. That way he wouldn't gain weight eating all the food these guys made. Maybe he would start working out with Brock, just to stay trim.

Dylan slathered peanut butter on bread, then poured all three of them glasses of milk.

They all sat together, eating hard before anyone started talking.

The first thing Rey wanted to know was "How's James?"

"Sleeping. I got him hooked up to some fluids, and he was pissed about that for about two seconds before he passed out." Kit winked. "He'll be fine. He took a hard concussive wave when the building dropped."

"I didn't run away," he told them. Rey needed the guys to understand. "James sent me to protect the safe. That's where I was when things started to go upside down."

He wasn't a coward. He wasn't.

"I know that, dork." Dylan rubbed his lower back. "He would have wanted to stay with his computers, but they were after the safe."

Mick wandered in, scratching his bare belly. He wore a pair of sweats, his chest fuzzy and wide. "I thought I smelled bread."

"I was hungry," Kit said softly.

Mick reached out and ruffled Kit's hair. "I love it when you get your baking on, kiddo."

Kit ducked his head and grinned. "I was itchy. You know how it is."

"Yeah, Brock and that Locke guy have been sparring for at least an hour."

"He's quite the bear," Rey said. He thought there was something going on between Locke and Brock, the way they looked at one another.

"God, yes." Kit flushed. They all looked at him. "I mean, he's a grizzly. That's impressive."

"I think Locke is a good friend, hmm?" Rey winked at Kit. "To Brock."

"Yeah. Apparently Locke and him go back a ways." Mick grinned. "I might hire him, if he sticks around. Brock says he was doing a lot of jobs out of town."

"Someone else we have to remember their name," Dylan grumbled.

"Brock calls him Griz. All of you just call me 'boss.'" Mick gave them all an impartial glare, including Rey.

Rey stared over. "Do I?"

"Yep." Mick licked jelly off his lower lip. "We need a guy with your skills."

Dylan hummed, hand sliding along his hip.

"Not those skills, Dylan." Kit laughed and laughed.

"No. Those skills belong to me now, little bear." Dylan sounded altogether pleased by that.

"Ew." Mick flapped a big hand. "I mean your information gathering and your, uh...."

"We don't need a psychic fox on the team," Brock said from the doorway, towel around his neck. When Rey met his gaze, though, his eyes were dancing. Laughing.

"Don't be stupid, Brock." Kit rolled his eyes. "Foxes can sense magnetic fields and vibrations in the earth. That's how they hunt."

"We do. I swear, I don't have visions. I hear things coming."

"Well, that's better than you being all weird." Brock gave him a broad wink. "Griz, this is what happens around here when Kit gets all het up. Food."

Locke peered into the kitchen, waving at them all. "Wow."

"I know, right?"

"Are y'all hiring? I am so tired of eating McDonald's."

"We actually are." Mick glanced at them all in turn. "Guys, I really would like to add Rey to the team, and I think Locke would be a great addition. We're going to have to find new offices, and we can get a place with room for all. Someplace harder to knock down than that wreck we have now."

Locke nodded easily. "There's some great space at the Stapleton complex still."

Rey searched Dylan's eyes, curious to what his mate said.

"I think it's a good idea, but I also like the idea of bolt holes like this one. We need to diversify, boss. I'm willing to stop renting somewhere else if you're willing to let me invest." Dylan rubbed his back, the touch soothing. "And I want my mate with me, of course."

"I said we were bringing him on." Mick looked at Rey. "What do you say, foxy?"

"If there's work for me, I'll do it. I'm good at what I do." He was exceptional, even.

"There will be plenty, sweetheart." Dylan hugged him close to one side of that big body, and Rey melted in. He loved the way Dylan smelled.

"Sweetheart?" Brock began gagging.

Locke whacked him on the shoulder. "Stop it. Twu wuv needs no mockery."

"Can we poison them, Kit?" Rey hid his grin in Dylan's arm.

"Yes. Let me get the rat poison for their cheese breads." Kit's chortle made everyone laugh.

"You made me *pão de queijo*?" Brock asked, sounding hopeful.

"I did." Kit handed over a basket. Brock looked... well, adorably surprised.

"Thanks, bear. You rock. You want one, foxy? They're full of cheesy goodness."

Rey snagged one, teeth sinking in. Oh. Goodness, Brock was right. Salty cheese and crispy bread, but soft in the middle, the bite was like magic.

"Brock likes those best," Locke murmured, watching Brock carefully.

Oh. Oh neat. That relationship was going to be fun to watch. Rey hugged Dylan's arm, then took another bite of cheese bread. What a weird and wonderful new den he was going to have.

Dylan kissed the top of his head. "Welcome home, Rey."

Welcome to the pack.

Epilogue

Mick knew the fox would be trouble the moment he walked in the door.

Now, how much trouble had been up for debate. It wasn't anymore. They'd sifted through the rubble of the old office, taken the insurance on, and agreed to testify against the crazy tiger....

Mick looked up at their new office and apartment building with utter satisfaction. The place had offices on the main floor, a gym in the lower level, and lofts on the second and third floors.

Rey had an office with James, an apartment with Dylan, and shared a huge communal kitchen with Kit. The guy fit in. Like, really. Even Brock adored him, and that was saying something.

"It's a good space, boss." Speaking of the sneaky little fox, he was right there, smiling up at the building.

"No bad vibes?"

"No, sir. I'll holler if I...." Rey's head tilted, the long nose twitching, which by now Mick understood. Something was coming.

Oh. Oh shit.

Yeah, the fox was trouble, all the way.

Thank goodness he was on the Apex team now.

Want More?

Join the Spurs and Shifters Newsletter for free stories, news, and contests from Julia Talbot and BA Tortuga!
    https://lp.constantcontact.com/su/A9CRUzp/baandjulia

Afterword

Hey, folks!

Thanks so much for reading my book! I'm so glad you made it here. If you liked the book, I hope you'll consider leaving a rating or review at your retailer of choice or adding the book to your Goodreads shelf.

If you're interested in more of my books, or in news about when they come out and what's coming soon, please check out my Facebook Group https://www.facebook.com/groups/juliatalbot/ or my newsletter here: https://lp.constantcontact.com/su/A9CRUzp/baandjulia

XXOO and Keep reading!

Julia Talbot

Also by Julia Talbot

Alpha Tales

An Alpha in Sheep's Clothing

Packmate for Hire

Too Many Alphas

Apex Investigations

Fox and Wolf

Jaguar and Grizzly

Mountain Lion and Bobcat

Alpha and Bear

Apex Security

Solids and Stripes

Dead and Breakfast

Fangs and Catnip

Fangs for the Memories

Home for the Howlidays

Full Moon Dating

New Moon

Isaiah and Jameson

Grizzly List

Bear Wanted

One and Only Bear

Bearly Working

Midnight Rodeo
Big Bear, Little Bear
Light a Rocket
Vampire Protection
The Dragon's Dilemma
Up in Flames

Nose to Tail, Inc.
Wolfmanny
Wolf's Man Friday
Wolf Maneuvers

The Peculiars
The Curse of the Mummy's Heart
The Shadow of the Count

Riding Cowboy Flats
Jackass Flats
Just a Cowboy
Riding the Circuit

Summit Springs
High Side

* * *

Contemporary
Catching Heir
Chef on Chef

Drive Your Truck

Home for the Hollandaise

Jumping, Landing, and Taking

Loose Snow

Love Dot Com

One More Yule Log

Out of the Frying Pan

Perfect

Sparkle and Shine

Historical

A Gentleman of Substance

A Pirate's Paradise

Offerings

Partners on the Trail

Post Obsession

Remembering Pleasure

To Hell You Ride

The White City

Paranormal

Bad Dog

Blue Moon Bar

Faster Bobcat

Link to the Crescent

Night of the Living Manny

Pack Mates

The Fire Inside

Thorns

Tomb of the God King

Touching Evil

About the Author

Julia Talbot lives in the great Southwest with her wife and four basset hounds. A full-time author, Julia writes paranormals and more with lots of love and action and, as her alter ego Minerva Howe, she writes mpreg and alpha/omega stories. She believes that everyone deserves a happy ending, so she writes about love without limits, where all of her stories leave a mark.

Visit Julia's website: http://www.juliatalbot.com